On Air

by Henry Fennell

TABLE OF CONTENTS

I remember it as the last time we tried to do something fun as a family. I was eight-years-old. My little sister, Ginny, was five-years-old. It was a simple thing, a picnic, on the banks of the river. It was just warm enough, not hot, and there was a pleasant breeze bringing the familiar smell of the river across the water and up to our picnic spot. My mother had fried chicken, made potato salad, and filled a glass jar with sweet tea and ice. She spread a red-checkered tablecloth on the ground under a stand of cottonwood trees overlooking a great expanse of the Mississippi River, and the four of us settled down to enjoy the meal and the view. Little was said between my father and mother, as we ate. My little sister seemed very happy, and I guess I was too.

I always looked forward to seeing the river. It was the most commanding and majestic thing that a young boy who never left this part of Tennessee could imagine. The road from our town dropped down a high bluff, then across a wide expanse of bottomland, over a big, rusty bridge that spanned a slough that people called Old River, and onto the Mississippi. You could feel the river, and then smell it, long before you could see it.

Blooms from the trees were sailing gently through the air around us, and once we were done eating, my little sister, Ginny, and I began to chase and grab as many as we could. We were having our fun, and I didn't take notice of what was happening between my parents. Whatever happened, whatever was said, it set my father off and put an end to the picnic.

He yelled at us to get in the station wagon. My

mother tried to gather up the remains of the picnic and he was having none of it. He ordered her to leave it and get in the car. We followed him; no one dared to look his way. We were all scared. He muttered something I couldn't understand and quickly pulled the car back onto the river road and sped towards town. He kept gathering speed as we neared Old River Bridge. I remember my mother saying "please" very softly and him ignoring her.

Old River Bridge was barely wide enough for two cars. Thin metal bars along each side provided the only barrier between the narrow road and a fall to the brown water below. We were going very fast—too fast—as our car lurched up onto the bridge. And maybe it would have been okay if an old logging truck had not reached the other end of the bridge at about the same time.

My father might have seen the truck in time to stop and let it pass, but he didn't, and he didn't slow down. I could see enough from the back seat to imagine our car and the truck crashing into each other, as we moved closer. Our car was moving in a line that crossed the center of the road. At the last second, my father jerked the steering wheel to the right, and then slightly back to the left. It gave us enough room to get by the truck without colliding, but it also sent us inches away from the thin railing of the bridge. I had time to look closely at the brown water below in the moment our car rubbed against a section of the rail that stuck out a little farther than the one before it. I saw sparks as the side of our car grinded into the rusty iron. My mother and Ginny screamed; I would have screamed too if I could have made a sound.

Chapter 1

The first time I saw the inside of a radio station was the day I went to work at one. At least I thought I was going to work there. I was nearly sixteen years old and the man who managed the radio station in Harper's Junction hired a couple of high school kids each year to work part-time. The kids he chose got a chance to announce on the radio, and a lot of kids wanted the job. My freshman English teacher knew him and recommended me for the job. I never asked her why she gave him my name.

WHJ Radio occupied a small space on the second floor of a building located on the town square in Harper's Junction. I was now climbing the stairs up to the studios to meet the station manager. I knew him from hearing him on the radio, but I had never met him. And though I'm sure I had seen him around town, I couldn't remember what he looked like. I pushed open the smoked glass door to go inside and was greeted with a stern look from a woman sitting behind a small desk, and she was smoking a cigarette.

"Can I help you?" she asked, without changing expression.

"I'm here to see Mr. Lawson," I answered softly.

"Is he expecting you?" she wanted to know.

"I think so."

"Woodrow!" she shouted down the hall. "There is a boy here to see you. Says you knew he was coming."

"Yeah, okay, give me a minute," came the answer from someone in the back.

"You heard him," she said to me. "Have a seat."

I sat down on a worn wooden chair across from her desk and waited. I tried not to look her in the eye. She was making me nervous, and I didn't want to seem nervous when the station manager came to get me. I read the plaques on the walls and looked at the photos hung around the place. There was a certificate from "The Association of Broadcasters" and one from "The Chamber of Commerce." Another said the station was a high school booster – one for sports and another for the band. There were photos of men standing with microphones in hand interviewing other men. One of the men being interviewed was the former governor. I didn't recognize the others.

I waited for a few minutes, but it seemed like longer. The woman behind the desk had time to light another cigarette before a small man with a perfect hair cut—kind of an early Beatles look—appeared from down the hall.

"You must be Neil," he said to me.

"Yes sir," I answered.

"You don't have to call me sir," he said. "Call me Woody."

"Yes…" I started to say sir. "Okay."

"You know I went to school with your mother," he told me. That was a surprise, a guy with a bit of a mod-looking hair cut was my mother's age."

"No..." I paused, wanting to say 'sir' again. "No, I didn't know that."

"Yeah, I liked your mother. Very nice girl, very pretty."

I was hoping he would stop there.

"How is she? I haven't seen her in a long while."

"She's okay, I guess. Yeah fine," I told him.

"Please tell her I said hello." I didn't answer. "So this

is WHJ, Neil," he said proudly. "Have you ever been here before?"

"No, I haven't," I answered. It didn't seem smart to tell him that I had never been inside of any radio station and had never been that curious about it either.

"Let me show you the place and then we can talk a little."

"Yes, sounds good."

I followed him down a short hallway past a small office on the left and towards two glass-enclosed booths on the right. I guess you could call them rooms. They were the size of large closets. The wood walls came up about three feet. Above them, large glass windows reached almost to the ceiling. The first room was empty. Woody propped open the door of the first small room and motioned me inside.

"This is the production room," he said. That meant nothing to me. "We record commercials and anything else we produce to go on the air in here." I nodded like I had some idea of what he was saying. The "record commercials" part made some sense. They had to come from somewhere, I thought. There was a microphone, a tape recorder, a turntable, a big piece of equipment with lots of switches and buttons on it, and a few other things that I did not recognize. All the equipment looked worn and well used. The place reeked of cigarette smoke. Woody picked up a thin, rectangular, plastic contraption from a pile of about twenty of the things and held it out for me to see.

"This is a cart," he said. "Cart, short for tape cartridge," he further explained. "See that, down in there?" he said, pointing through the clear plastic top of the "cart" at some thin brown tape inside. "That's tape. That's recording tape that's been put into a loop." It occurred to me that this might be my first radio lesson, so I tried to pay closer attention.

He pointed out a few other things in the room. He called the big piece of equipment with all the switches and dials the board. "It all comes through the board," he said. "All the sound goes into the board and then leaves. My voice goes in through the microphone and then it comes out of the board to the tape recorder," he told me by example. "Some people might call this a mixing board. In radio, we just call it the board. There's another one, a bigger one, in the control room that I'll show you." First lesson: The board is very important, so far the most important thing in the radio station.

We walked out the production room and he asked me to follow him into the glass-enclosed room next door. The small room had a sign hung outside the door that said, "On Air". Woody warned me to "never open this door if that sign is on." He said it in such a way that I was sure I would never forget it. *Open this door when this light is on and something really bad could happen*, I thought. The light wasn't on, so he opened the door and the two of us stepped inside. The room looked a lot like the other one, but with more stuff. There was more equipment – a bigger board, more cart machines, more turntables, more microphones, a little more space, and a big window that looked out over the town square. And there was a man sitting in a chair facing the board. He turned around and looked directly at me. He was not happy to see me standing there. He reached back toward the board and twisted a big knob that turned down the music that was playing.

"Billy, this is Neil," Woody said to the man sitting there. He muttered "hey" and didn't reach out to shake my hand. "I'm showing him around. He might be helping us out."

7

Billy said nothing and turned around to face a microphone hanging from a long arm that was attached somewhere behind the board. I took note that he said, "might be helping us out." That was my first hint that me working here wasn't a done deal.

Billy picked up some headphones that were lying in front of the board and slipped them over his head. Woody looked over at me and made a "quiet" gesture by putting his finger up to his mouth. The two of us stood there silently for several seconds, watching Billy from behind. He reached over to the far left of the board and flipped a switch to the right. The music shut off and he waited another couple of seconds before turning the knob below that switch.

"WHJ!" Billy shouted into the microphone and towards the wall in the front of him. This fellow who had barely made a sound before was now yelling inside a small glass enclosed closet and it was loud. "That's Todd Rundgren and 'I Saw the Light in Your Eyes'. It's seventy-eight degrees at 10:22 in the morning. I'm Billy Brown and here's new music from a new group. They call themselves The Eagles and this is 'Take it Easy'."

I listened to the radio a lot, and I had probably seen radio announcers in movies, but I had never pictured this scene—a man in a very small room perched over the town square, talking very loudly and unnaturally at no one in front of him. It struck me as pretty funny, and I smiled. Woody noticed me smiling and I think he took it to mean that I thought what I was hearing and seeing was pretty neat. I didn't. I thought it was weird.

Billy flipped the switch on the board that he had used before he began talking and sat his headphones down in front of him. Without acknowledging us again, he picked up a clipboard lying beside him and began to study the sheet of paper attached to it.

"Let's get out of here and let Billy work," Woody suggested, and we turned to go out the door. I figured I should use some manners and told Billy "nice to meet you." He might have grunted something in return, but I wasn't sure.

"We call that the control room," Woody said as he closed the door behind us. "You might hear some people call it the announcer's booth. The thing to remember is whatever goes out on the control room goes on the radio. You say something into the microphone in there and people hear it on WHJ, and you can't take it back. You play something on tape in there and it goes on the radio. That's the first thing to remember about the control room—never say anything through the microphone or play anything through the board that you don't want, or we don't want heard on the radio. Okay?" he told me.

"I understand," I said, and I think I did understand. I knew there were certain things you could not say on the radio. I didn't' know exactly what things you couldn't say or why you couldn't say them, but at least I kind of got the idea.

Woody opened another door just outside the control room and pointed to a big metal machine inside. It was shaped like the large mailboxes you see on the street, but not quite as big, and it had a glass window at the top. I could see what looked like typewriter keys inside. Long sheets of yellow paper with typewriting on them hung from nails on the walls of the small, closet-like space around the machine. Signs above the nails read "National", "State", "Sports", and "Weather".

"This is our wire machine," Woody said to me. "We get a lot of our news off the wire. You see those signs? Those are stories that we might use later. Part of Billy's job right now is to clear the wire machine and make sure it does not run out of paper. Very important," he said. Woody had lost me. I needed more information. Moments later the big machine began to hum; seconds after that it began to type on its own. Typewriter-like keys struck the paper on the roll very quickly, and the roll unwound with lines and lines of sentences, and dates, and markings I had never seen. My mind went back to things I had seen on television and in the movies—people in newspaper offices and telegraph offices watching words being typed as if by magic on machines like this one.

Woody watched the machine work and the paper roll out for a couple of minutes before reaching down and severing a couple of feet of the now type-covered paper with a swipe of the nail on his index finger across a small ridge on the front of the machine. The paper came off nice and neat. He held it up and studied it for just a couple of seconds. "These are state headlines," he explained. "Billy will be using some of these at the top of the hour. We don't just play records. We read the news too. We're full service around here. Woody pinned the sheet he was holding on the nail below the "State" sign and looked around at some of the other pieces of paper hung on the various nails. He pulled some of the printed pages down from under the National, Sports, and Weather signs and said, "Billy won't need these."

I followed him back down the short hallway and around to a larger room that faced the two booths we were just in. Woody turned on the lights and told me that this was the studio. There was a small desk in one corner and a piano in the opposite corner across from the control room we had just been in. Between the two, a set of wooden bookshelves held hundreds of records. A small table with a microphone and a couple of tape players sat next to the glass facing the control room. And just like the control room, there was a large glass window looking out over the town square.

That was it. That was WHJ—two tiny rooms, one slightly larger room, a closet with a wire machine, a small office, and a couple of big windows that looked over the Harper's Junction town square. Radio seemed much bigger than that from the outside. I followed Woody into his office and sat down in one of the two wooden chairs that faced his desk. His desk was strewn with papers and a few records. He sat down in his larger, cushioned chair and pulled a pack of cigarettes from the middle drawer of the desk. I studied the office a little bit, while he opened the pack and lit a cigarette. There were several photographs of Woody on the wall. One showed him in a control room with his headphones on, looking like he was talking into the microphone. Another photo pictured him standing next to a boy in a football uniform. Woody was holding a microphone up near the boy's mouth. I recognized the boy. He was several years older than me, but I knew him as the star quarterback on one of Harper's Junction's best football teams. And there was a photo of Woody and three other men holding golf clubs.

Woody got a cigarette going and leaned back in his chair. "Neil this is an important job, especially for a young man like yourself. A lot of people around here depend on us and we don't let just anybody do this. There's too much at stake," he explained to me. I nodded, and he continued. "I'm going to give you some copy to take home. I want you to practice reading it out loud like you would if you were on the radio. And while you're at it, I want you to listen to the radio.

Listen closely and think about what the person is saying and doing. If you want to do this, that's the most important thing—what's being said and how it's being said. How do you sound to someone listening?" He took a long draw off his cigarette and blew the smoke up towards the ceiling.

"We can teach how to operate the place. They tell me you're pretty smart, so that won't be a problem. I want to know how you're going to sound. Okay?" he said.

I started to answer, "yes sir" again, but managed to say "okay."

"Don't worry about being perfect right from the start. You'll get better," he added. "Come back up here on Wednesday afternoon and I'll record you reading this copy. You know we've got a couple of kids going off to college this fall, and I'll need to replace them. I need to have somebody ready to go soon. You work on this and do your best, and we'll see if we can work things out with you."

I told him I would work hard and do my best. He got up from behind his desk and shook my hand. Then he handed me the copy and told me he would see me Wednesday after school. I thanked him and walked out of his office. I passed the woman sitting out front. I figured I should thank her too. "Thanks," I said. "I'll see you Wednesday." She looked at me without expression and answered, "yeah, okay."

I went down the stairs, out the door, and onto the sidewalk that stretched around the square. It was mid-afternoon, and I figured that a couple of my buddies would probably be working at their part-time jobs on the square. I crossed the street and made a straight line through the courthouse lawn to Geist's Drug Store. Ben and Coy might be there, and I was also hoping that I would see Angie. She worked the soda fountain after school some days. I checked my pockets to see if I had enough money to order something if she was in there. I didn't have enough, so I thought about what I might say to her to start a conversation without ordering. I opened the double glass door to the drug store and looked inside. Angie was there, but I didn't see Ben or Coy.

"Hey Angie," I said to her. "I was kind of looking for Ben and Coy. Are they here?"

"I think they are on a delivery," she answered.

"Both of them?" I asked, knowing that there was only the one truck that Geist used for deliveries, and it didn't take two people to deliver prescriptions.

"You know them. They run off together whenever they can. They're out somewhere goofing off. Ben thinks he can get away with it because his daddy is the boss."

"Yeah, I guess so. How long are you working?"

"I'll be here until closing. You want something?"

I pretended like I was thinking about ordering for a few moments, knowing I didn't have the money.

"I don't think so. I'm not really thirsty."

I stood and looked across at her standing behind the fountain while I tried to come up with something interesting to say.

"So, are you going to be working a lot this summer?" I asked her.

"I hope so. I guess it's better than sitting around the house, and I like the extra money. What about you? Will you be working at the store?"

She was talking about the little grocery store that my mother ran. I had worked there ever since she opened it a few years back. I was tired of being there, and it was the main reason I had considered talking to someone about working at a radio station. I saw it as a chance to get out of the store. My mother had agreed to let me talk to Woody about the job, even though she needed my help. It felt selfish of me, but she seemed to think it might be a good thing.

"I might not be. I'm not sure." I was fumbling around for the right thing to say, not at all sure that I should bring up the radio job to Angie. I had just been told that it might not be a sure thing. I would look real stupid if I told her about it and then it didn't happen, but I couldn't help myself.

"I think I'm getting a job at the radio station," I blurted out.

Angie got a curious look on her face.

"At the radio station?"

"Yeah, I just talked to Woody Lawson. A couple of guys, you know Rusty and Chris, are going off to college, and he needs somebody."

"Wow," she interrupted. "The radio station. You're going to work at the radio station."

I tried to slow her down. "Well, I just talked to him. I think so. We've still got some things to work out."

"I wonder how you will sound on the radio?" she asked.

It was a good question and I had no answer, not even a clue. Guess I will find out Wednesday, I thought. I shrugged and Angie smiled.

"I wonder," she said again. "Looks like the Bobbsey Twins are back," Angie nodded toward the front window of the store. It was Ben and Coy. They had parked the delivery truck in front of the store and were coming inside. "You two manage to get those prescriptions delivered?" she kidded. "Maybe Neil can come along too. It might take three of you next time."

"We would send you," Ben shot back, "but that would put everybody around here in danger, the way you drive." Angie started to protest, but let it drop.

"Neil says he's gonna be on the radio," Angie told the two of them.

"You didn't tell me that," Coy said to me.

"There's not much to tell yet. I talked to the guy, Woody Lawson. They're gonna need somebody starting sometime this summer. I don't know if I have the job or not, maybe."

"What do you mean?' Ben asked.

"Well, there's kind of a tryout, I guess," I said, holding up the rolled-up paper in my hand. "He wants me to read this for him, then I guess he'll decide. I'm not sure."

"Well that's something," Ben said. "On the radio huh? You should think about a radio name."

"I don't think so," I answered.

"Yeah, something like 'Neil The Real Deal Robinson'."

"That sucks," Coy said. "Sounds like a wrestler's name."

"Awful," I said. "I don't think any of these guys change their names anyway. I'm sure I won't."

"Neil The Real Deal," Ben repeated. "Think about it."

"I'm sure I won't think about it."

"I think it's pretty exciting, Neil on the radio," Angie said. I smiled, but I was getting a little anxious about the whole thing. I wasn't on the radio yet, far from it. Now I knew I should have waited to say anything about it, but it was too late. I did like the way Angie reacted. It was my first hint that she might find me a little more interesting if I was on the radio. They probably wouldn't though, if I were really bad at it.

Ben's father, the pharmacist, called him and Coy to the back of the store, leaving Angie and me alone up front.

"It really does sound like a fun job," Angie said. "Sure beats working at the soda fountain."

"I don't know about that. It might not happen, and I might be terrible at it," I told her.

"Oh! I think you'll be really good Neil," she said. She didn't have to say it, and of course she didn't have a clue if I would be good on the radio, but it was very nice of her. I should have told her how nice it was. Instead, I just said, "Hope so."

Ben and Coy got busy cleaning and straightening up around the store, and Angie got a couple of customers, so I left and started walking home. The walk gave me some time to think. The radio station thing was a lot more real now. I looked at it mainly as a way to get out of working at the store. Now, I was going to have to figure out how to do the job if I really wanted it. I hoped Woody was right about the equipment, about it not being all that hard to learn to operate. It all looked complicated to me. I had never even seen anything like it, much less try to operate it. Hopefully, I would feel better about it when I got going. That is if I got going.

Momma was sitting in her chair behind the cash register when I got to the store. She was smoking a cigarette. There were no customers. I got a coke, opened it on the side of the cooler, and sat down on the stool near her chair.

"What happened?" she wanted to know, first thing.

"He wants me to come back Wednesday after school and record some of this stuff he gave me," I said, and held the rolled-up paper out for her to see.

"What is it?"

"News mostly, I guess, and some other stuff," I

answered.

"And you're suppose to record it. What does that mean?"

"I watched him record some things he said into a microphone. That's what he wants me to do," I said, trying to explain something I didn't much understand.

"When do you start work then?" she asked me.

"That's the thing. I'm not sure. He wants to hear how I sound, and then, I don't know, I guess I'll have to learn the rest."

"What else happened?"

"The woman at the front desk didn't have much to say to me. She didn't seem very nice," I told Momma.

"That's Louise Burns. She's all right. Known her all my life," Momma said. "You just need to get to know her a little bit."

"The man on the radio, Billy, wasn't nice either."

"I've heard him on there. What did he say to you?"

"Nothing really, he wouldn't even look at me."

"Maybe he was just busy," she said. "What about Woody?"

I thought for a moment about telling her that he said hello, but I didn't.

"He was okay. He seems like a nice enough man, told me to call him Woody and not to worry about 'yes sir' and all that."

"Hmmm," she said. "Maybe you should call him sir anyway."

"I don't think so. He sounded pretty plain about it," I answered.

"Well, still. You need to be polite to him and to

Louise. This is your first real job Neil. You want to make a good impression."

"Yes ma'am. I will. I'll try to."

"That won't be hard for you," she said, encouraging me.

I stayed with her in the store until closing and worked the checkout counter and cash register. Between customers, I began to read over the stories Woody had given me. I read them to myself at first and then began reading out loud, softly but loud enough where I could hear myself. I tried to think about how the guys on radio and television sounded when they were reading the news, but to me I was sounding more like someone reading a book report out loud in class.

We closed the store at six o'clock. She counted the money and locked up. I walked across the street to our house. Momma took the little green bank bag with the day's receipts inside out to her car and drove the hundred yards or so from the store parking lot, across the street, and into the driveway behind our house.

Ginny was there when I got home. She turned off the television when I came in and was pretending to be doing homework by the time my mother walked in.

"How close are you to finishing?" Momma asked her about her homework.

"Almost," she answered. I knew she hadn't even started. My little sister was in the sixth grade, and she could always make up excuses to get out of helping at the store. She must have told our mother she had a lot of homework so she could stay home, talk on the phone, and watch television.

"What about you Neil?"

"I don't have very much," I answered, giving her one

of my usual answers whether I had a lot of homework or not. She didn't look convinced.

"Be sure and get it done. You need to get your grades up."

She reminded me quite a bit about "getting my grades up." She was right of course, especially about Algebra. Algebra started off pretty easy, but it had gotten harder towards the end of the school year. It got harder, but I hadn't worked harder. There was even a chance I could flunk Algebra with another bad six-weeks grade and a bad final exam. I couldn't even think about it. It was painful to even imagine having to take algebra again with a bunch of younger kids. I couldn't let that happen.

Momma fixed sandwiches for the three of us, and we sat at the kitchen table to eat. Ginny asked me about the radio station, and I repeated what I had told our mother about having to record some stuff.

"I don't know what you would sound like on the radio," she said, and kind of looked like she was trying to imagine it. "You wouldn't sound like anyone I know. They all sound grown. You're not grown."

"No Ginny. I'm not grown, but I'm not a baby either," I said to her. "I'll sound all right." I said it, but I really had no idea.

"So, you're gonna play records, right?" she asked.

"I guess so—play records, read the news, whatever they do, that's what I'll do."

"The guys on WHBQ play the best music. WHJ doesn't play as much good music," she said.

"It's not WHBQ. It's not Memphis. It's Harper's Junction. It's different," I tried to explain to her, not really understanding it myself.

"Why?" she asked.

"Because WHBQ is Memphis; WHJ is Harper's Junction. I don't know," I said.

"Ginny, there is nothing wrong with WHJ. I think they do a good job with all the local news they read in the morning," Momma said.

I hadn't thought much about the local news on WHJ. I didn't listen to it very much, so I wasn't sure why people in town would listen. I listened to the radio stations in Memphis, just like Ginny did. At night, I listened to stations from Chicago for music, or a station in St. Louis for Cardinals baseball. I guess my mother really knew more about who listened to WHJ, and why they listened to it, than I did.

I went back to my bedroom after supper with the paper from the radio station and lay down on my bed. I propped myself up on some pillows and held the copy up to read over some more. There was a story about a Ford car called the Torino that had been recalled because it had bad axles. I had some idea of what that meant, but I wondered what would happen to the cars. Another story talked about the astronauts on Apollo 16 preparing to go to the moon. They were scheduled to walk on the moon Friday. I knew a lot about the first moonwalk in 1969. I watched it on television, but now I knew almost nothing about this one coming up. There was a story about George McGovern and the democratic presidential primaries, and another about President Nixon's plans to withdraw more troops from Vietnam. The last story was about a new camera that developed photos "right before your eyes."

I knew something about the news, maybe more than some other kids my age. I liked to read the newspaper and watch the evening television news, but I didn't think I knew enough to talk about the news on the radio. I hoped that wouldn't be a big part of the job at the station. I read the stories again, out loud, and tried to imagine how to sound like a newsman. I wasn't confident, and I had no sense of the way I sounded.

I put the copy down and picked up my Algebra book. There were three weeks of school left, and I was behind. I looked at the problems that had been assigned, and I wasn't even sure how to start a couple of them. This was the hardest stuff we had been given—linear equations and quadratic equations—and I hadn't been paying attention or working through all the problems as I should have. I started work on a couple of problems and then put them aside without finishing either one of them. Three weeks, I tried to convince myself that I could catch up enough in that much time. Then I promised myself to pay attention in class the next day.

I went back in the living room and told my mother I had finished my homework. We sat and watched television together for a couple of hours, *Here's Lucy* and *The Doris Day Show*. Momma liked those shows. Then we watched my new favorite, *The Sonny and Cher Comedy Hour*. It was a hipper show. They talked about things from the 60s and 70s, and Cher showed her belly button. Sonny couldn't sing very well, but that didn't bother me. I was surprised that my mother seemed to enjoy it too. We watched the whole thing together, before I went to bed.

I was hoping to go to sleep before my father got home. He almost always came home late. He barely stayed at our house—out early, back late at night, or sometimes not at all. I might see him on the weekend, but as it was now I didn't want to see him at all. Of course the harder I tried to get to sleep, the harder it was to fall asleep. I was still awake when the back door opened and he came in the house. It was late, but my mother was still sitting on the couch with the television on. Luckily, they didn't speak to one another. If they had spoken, it would have been an argument, yelling, or worse. He came straight back to their bedroom. I heard him fumble around for a while and then fall into bed. That was the best I could have hoped for.

Chapter 2

I got a ride with Ben up to the square on Wednesday after school. I had my audition copy folded up in a school notebook. He dropped me off in front of the radio station.

"Go get 'em Real Deal," he yelled out his car window at me.

"Screw you," I yelled back at him. He laughed and pulled away.

I went inside and headed up the stairs towards the studios. I had a couple of schoolbooks with me, along with the notebook. For whatever reason, I didn't think I should take the books inside, so I went back down and sat them at the bottom of the stairs. I walked up the stairs again and tried to clear my throat before stepping inside.

The woman, Mrs. Burns, was sitting at her desk when I opened the door. She was in the same position as the other day, with what looked like the same cigarette going, and wearing the same expression. I said hello. Instead of saying hello back she yelled:

"Woodrow, the boy is here!" She called him Woodrow instead of Woody for some reason. Woody called me into his office and I thanked Mrs. Burns. She smiled slightly.

"You ready to record?" he asked me.

"I think so; I hope so," I tried to say with a smile.

"Well let's do it," he said, and led me out of his office and into the production room. I stood and watched as he put a reel of tape on the machine next to the board. He threaded the tape through an opening in the middle of the machine and wound the end onto an empty reel on the other side. He pushed a couple of buttons and gestured for me to sit down in front of the microphone.

"Here, try these on," he said, as he picked up a pair of headphones and slipped them over my ears. "That okay?" he asked. I nodded yes, but of course I didn't know if they were okay or not.

Woody reached over to the switch on the far left side of the board and flipped it to the right. When he did, I could hear the sound coming from the headphones.

"Read a little bit and I'll set your levels." I wasn't sure what he meant and he picked up on that. "Read some of your copy out loud, and I'll adjust your microphone level so you can record."

Okay, read out loud, I thought. I was just hoping some sound would come out. My mouth and throat suddenly felt completely dry. I licked my lips and tried to get some spit going. Holding the paper in front of my eyes and trying not to shake so much that Woody would notice. I started to read. I could hear myself in the headphones, so I figured I was at least making some sound. It was also very distracting. I didn't know whether to try and listen to myself in the headphones, or what, so I kept pausing.

"The Ford Motor Company…has recalled over 200,000…of its Torino models. Ford believes the axles…on the cars…"

Woody interrupted. "Just read straight through," he said. "Your level is okay. Read those six stories. You can pause between the stories, but not so much during them. Remember to speak up. All right?"

"Yes," I started to say sir again. "Okay, I will."

"When you're ready, start the tape. Just push this," he

said gesturing to a red button on the machine. "Come and get me when you're done."

He closed the door, and I stared at the red button. It was very quiet in the room, and I could hear my heart beating quickly in my ears. I took several deep breaths and started to push the button, but I couldn't make myself do it yet. I looked over the copy again and read some of it out loud, trying to get up the nerve to start. I figured I should start soon or Woody would think something was wrong. I took another big gulp of air and started the recorder.

I read through the stories pretty quickly, with just a few mistakes, I thought. I tried to speak loudly, louder than normal, and I tried to sound older, though I really didn't know how to accomplish that. I wasn't sure what to do when I was finished, so I took off the headphones and let the machine continue to run while I went to get Woody. He was in his office.

"All done?" he asked me. I nodded yes. "Well, let's see what we've got." We walked back around the corner and into the production room. Woody quickly rewound the tape, stopping it where my recording began. "Here we go," he said as he started the tape.

Something that sounded a little like I imagined my voice might sound came out of the speaker. The voice I heard cracked almost immediately. Then I heard myself stumble over the title and name of Secretary of State Henry Kissinger. It was embarrassing, and it didn't get much better as the recording went along. I messed up a few more words—all words that I knew perfectly well and should have been able to say easily. I was also reading faster, then slower, at different points for no reason. And my attempt to sound older just made me sound like a kid trying to sound old, and it all sounded bad to me.

My recording ended, and Woody stopped the tape.

"Not bad," he said. "You need to work on it though, a lot," he quickly added. "I want you to start listening to the radio as much as you can, and practice doing what you hear us doing, okay?" I nodded yes. "Say it out loud; read out loud. Don't be shy about it."

"I understand," I answered.

"You've got some time to learn before I need somebody. Chris will be here most of the summer, and I think he will help you learn the job before he leaves. You can come up and watch him. Sound okay?" he asked.

"Sounds great," I said, but I didn't know if it was great or not. I think he was saying I needed to get better before he would let me on the radio, and I would be learning how to do the job from a person I hardly knew.

"I'll tell Chris, and I'll get you the number to the control room. You can let him know when he's on the radio in the evenings or the weekends that you want to come up and watch, and he'll let you in."

Woody left the production room and grabbed some more wire copy to give me on the way out to practice with. He also wanted to show me something at the top of the steps. We walked out past Mrs. Burns. I looked over at her just in case she decided to look up from her desk and say something to me. She didn't. We stepped outside the door and Woody pointed to a pair of light switches on the wall.

"This top switch is the light for the steps. The one below it turns on a little red light in the control room. If you come up here without a key, and you want to get in, flip this switch a couple of times and the announcer will see it and come let you in," he explained. I thought that was pretty neat—a secret red light. I felt a little more like an insider, knowing about it.

Woody said goodbye, and I headed down the steps and out towards the square. "Don't forget your books," I heard him yell from the top of the stairs. He saw them sitting on the steps. I had forgotten to pick them up on the way out. "Thanks," I called back up to him. I felt silly since, for whatever reason, I was trying not to look like a high school kid. I picked up the books without looking back up at him and left the building.

I should have gone home to help out at the store, but my first thought was to walk across the square to the drugstore and see if Angie was working. Ben and Coy could be there too. They might want to hear what happened, and I hoped Angie would still be interested in what I was doing.

She was there. Angie was sitting on a stool behind the soda fountain when I walked in. She smiled when she saw me, and of course that made me smile too.

"Have you been back to WHJ?" she asked first thing.

"I was just there," I answered. She smiled again.

"Tell me what happened," she said.

I went through the whole thing about the audition and what it sounded like to me. I told her what Woody said and what I was supposed to do next. She listened and nodded, while smiling the whole time I talked. I tried to make it sound like it went pretty well.

"That sounds great, Neil," she said when I was finished telling her what happened. I tried to downplay it a little. From what Woody had said, I was not convinced that I would ever be on the radio.

"I don't know, Angie," I answered. "It's not a sure thing at all. I've got a lot to learn."

"No, I believe you're going to do this, and you're going to be good at it," she said confidently.

"I hope you're right," I answered, trying not to sound too doubtful.

We talked a little longer, before I had to tell her it was time for me to get to the store.

"If you're working on the square this summer, we'll probably be seeing each other more often," she said as I left.

What I should have said was "I hope so." What I said was "I guess so."

I thought about it all the way home. How could I let that pass? I tried to figure out how I could bring it up and correct it next time I saw her. I ran the imagined conversation through my head.

"I thought about what you said the other day, I would say. "I hope our schedules work out where we can see each other. I like talking to you." No, I would never really say that. I thought of several other ways to bring it up, but none of them sounded right. Probably the thing to do was to just keep talking to her, somehow. That made more sense than anything.

I was thinking about all that while walking down the street and didn't hear the pickup truck pull up behind me. Without warning, someone laid on the horn just a few feet from where I was walking, and I nearly screamed. My heart jumped in my chest and blood rushed to my head. I turned quickly to see what it was.

"Dammit Ben!" I screamed at the truck when I saw who was driving. He was driving his father's delivery truck and Coy was with him. They were laughing uncontrollably.

"Man you jumped," Coy said, as Ben pulled the truck up beside where I was standing.

"I guess so, you idiot," I answered.

"No reason to get mad about it," Ben said from the driver's side.

"Yeah, no reason, right," I said. Coy scooted over and I got in the truck.

"So, are you gonna be the new Mouth of the South?" Ben asked as we took off.

"You can do better than that," I answered.

"You didn't like The Real Deal. I'll have to work on it. What did he say? Did you get the job?"

"Maybe," I answered. I told them what happened and that I would be training with Chris.

"Chris is alright," Coy said. Ben pulled the truck up to our grocery store and let me out.

"Maybe y'all should try to do some work today and stop running around burning your daddy's gas," I said, trying to get a little dig in on the two of them

"That means a lot coming from the new Mouth of the South," Ben teased as he pulled away. The two of them laughed again, and I went inside to talk to my mother.

The store was empty of customers. My mother was standing behind the counter looking at receipts. I went to put my books down and saw my grandmother sitting in the big chair near the cash register. It was not unusual for her to come and sit with my mother since my grandfather died a couple of year ago. She grinned when she saw me. I was always glad to see her too. She was someone who seemed to calm things down, and she always had something good to say. I can't recall a real mean thing she ever said about anyone.

"How did it go?" Momma asked.

"It was okay, I think."

"Do you have the job?"

"He told me to start coming to the radio station for training."

"Will you get paid?"

"I didn't ask. I don't know. He didn't say anything about getting paid. Maybe you don't get paid for training," I said to her.

"Seems like you should," she answered.

"That's wonderful," my grandmother said, trying to take the focus off whether I was going to get paid right away. "You'll be on the radio soon and people all over the county will hear you. That's really something, Neil."

"Yeah, thanks Nana, but I'm not sure yet how this is going to turn out," I said.

"Well I'm sure it is going to turn out just fine. You're a smart boy, a good boy. People will like hearing you on the radio."

"I hope so. It doesn't seem real to me yet."

Momma asked when I was starting, and I told her I thought I would be going up to the radio station pretty soon.

"You need to talk to your daddy about this," she told me.

"Why don't you talk to him?" I quickly suggested.

"I've already talked to him about it, but you're going to have to say something. He's going to be mad if you don't, and you don't want that."

"He's going to be mad anyway, and it won't matter what I say to him. He won't like it," I answered. I had stopped trying to figure out why he was irritated. For whatever reason, he didn't want to be around us, and it was better for us when he wasn't.

"If you don't talk to him, he might not let you do this. And it won't matter what I say," Momma said.

She was right, trying to avoid him would just make things worse when it did come up. Either way, he would pretend to know why the idea of me working at the radio station was not a good one, and he would make it hard for me to feel good or confident about it. More and more, I was most interested in avoiding him all together.

We finished out the day at the store, and Momma took Nana home while I walked over to our house. Ginny was there, talking on the phone with the television on. She saw me, and kept on talking. I went back to my bedroom, lay down and replayed what happened at the radio station. It hadn't gone as well as I hoped. When I heard myself, it didn't sound like someone who should be on the radio, and I wondered what Woody really thought. I figured I could get better with practice, but I didn't know how much better, and I sure didn't know if it would be good enough to get me on the radio. It would have been better, I thought, if my friends didn't know about the job. That way if it didn't happen, if I didn't make it on the radio, no one would know the difference, and it wouldn't matter to anyone but me. Of course it was too late for that. My friends would know if I couldn't do this.

I stayed in my room for a while and started work on a couple of Algebra problems, but I didn't get very far. I was going to need a favor from Ben before final exams. He could help me catch up a little bit, and hopefully get me through the test. He would be pretty good about it too. He liked to kid, but he was not a jerk, and he was very smart. I put the homework aside and went out to sit with my mother. She was on the couch smoking a cigarette and watching *The Carol Burnett Show*.

"Finish your homework?" she asked. I lied and said yes.

We sat quietly and watched the show. I was barely watching, instead I was replaying the things Woody had said to me at the radio station, again. Today, just like the other day, he told me I should listen to the radio a lot. I hadn't been. When I did listen to the radio, it was to the Memphis stations. They had the best music and the best DJ's. I knew I needed to listen to WHJ, and I needed a new radio, a new transistor radio that I could carry around with me, one with an earpiece so I could listen anywhere and not bother people. I told my mother, and she said she would give me the money to buy one. That meant I could spend some time on the square tomorrow looking for a radio, and it would give me a good excuse to stop by and see Angie.

I went to bed thinking about all of that—the job, Algebra, and Angie. I also thought about the money I might make. It would be my first real paying job, and it might help me get a car. That would be something. The thought made me want to work as hard as possible to get the job. I was running all that around in my mind when I heard the back door open. It was my father, and he didn't go straight to his room. He went into the living room and started talking loudly to my mother.

I could tell right away that he had been drinking. He stayed out late and drank most nights. I wasn't sure what else he did when he was gone, but he was hardly ever around. If we were lucky, he would come home and fall into bed. If we weren't so lucky, on nights like this, he would come home angry and raise hell with my mother.

He was yelling now. I put my pillow over my head and tried not to hear, but it was impossible. He got louder, and he sounded madder by the minute. I heard him say my name at one point. He was mad about this job I was trying to get. He told her that I had no business at a radio station, and that I was supposed to help her at the store. I knew that wasn't the reason he was mad. He sure didn't care if she had help or not. She tried to tell him that it was okay with her, and she believed it would be good for me.

He began to swear and to threaten her and me. This was how it happened around our house at least once or twice a week—an angry drunk man I hardly knew, talking about killing me and my mother. It kept on like that until he seemed to run out of steam and stumbled back towards his bedroom. I tried to be as still and as quiet as possible as he passed my bedroom door. I watched the doorknob, hoping it wouldn't turn, and that I wouldn't see his face at my door. And as usual, I prayed for the strength to kill him before he killed me. I also prayed for him to die before it came to that. Those were my only two prayers.

Chapter 3

There were only three weeks of school left, and I was getting more anxious and angrier for falling behind in Algebra class. Our teacher knew several other kids in class were in the same shape, and he was getting more frustrated with us. He was trying to finish up, and we were trying to catch up, especially for the final exam. He went back and forth between some new problems and some old stuff that he had tried to teach early in the semester. He was blaming us for being behind, and he was mostly right about that. I hadn't been doing my part.

"Some of you need to buckle down and work a lot harder than you are now, or you're not going to make it out of this class," he announced just before the bell rang. "I want to see all your work tomorrow."

Ben and Coy sat near me in class. Ben was unbothered. He knew how to work all the problems, and it seemed to come easily to him. Coy was somewhere between Ben and me. He would probably want and need help before the final too, but not as much as me. I made some notes and tried to understand enough to do the assignment, but I knew it wouldn't be enough. When class ended, I walked out with Ben and Coy.

"Y'all want to get together tonight and do these problems?" I asked. Ben didn't say anything. He knew why I was asking. I was hoping Coy would join in, so it wouldn't be just me wanting help.

"I think that's a good idea. I could use the help." Coy said, and I was relieved.

"I've got to work closing. Seven-thirty, my house?" Ben suggested.

"Yeah, see you," I said.

It looked like rain when school let out. I should have gotten a ride to the square with Ben or Coy, but they had gotten away quickly. I started walking towards the square. It was only half a mile, but it was frustrating to be nearly sixteen years old and still walking. Several of the kids in my class who worked had cars, and so did a few other kids whose parents had enough money to buy one for them. I walked and thought about getting a car. It really didn't matter what kind of car— any car would be great. Ben drove a car that had belonged to his father. Coy drove an old truck that his grandfather had left him. He loved his truck. I was still riding the bus to school in the morning and getting rides where I could in the afternoon. Hopefully, that would change if I really did get this job.

It began to rain. I walked faster, hoping to get to the square before it got worse. The rain got heavier, and it began to thunder in the distance. I looked around for someplace to get out of the weather. I started to cross the street and climb up on the front porch of someone's house that I knew. I looked down the street before crossing and saw a blue Chevrolet coming. The car slowed down and stopped where I was standing. The driver cracked the window slightly and yelled out "Get in!" It was Angie. I ran around and got in just as the sky lit up and thunder rolled in close behind us.

"I'm wet," I said, apologizing before sitting on the seat of her car.

"I don't care," she said, smiling over at me. "Where you going?"

"The square," I answered.

"Good, I'm going to work. Are you going to the radio station?"

"I don't think so, not today, probably soon," I said.

"You don't know when you're starting?"

"I haven't worked it out with the guys yet, maybe this weekend or next weekend," I answered. I was surprised at how interested she seemed, but I liked it.

"I'm going to buy a new radio today, so I can listen to WHJ more."

"Oh," was all she said to that.

I looked around her car, and I looked more closely at her. Angie dressed nicer than most of the girls in our class. It was because of her job. She served customers at the soda fountain, but she also ran the cash register in the back sometimes. She looked and sounded very mature for her age. Today, she was wearing a brown dress with a wide white belt. She looked really good. I could have told her that, but I didn't.

"Is this your car?" I asked her.

"Not really. It's my mother's car, but she lets me drive it as much as I need to," she answered.

"I've been thinking about getting a car," I said, kind of boldly.

"So you're going to then?" she asked.

"If I get this job going, I should be able to get one," I said, still overstating the possibility.

"You'll probably need a car then," she said. "Going back and forth to work."

"That's what I thought," I answered. Having a car to drive was so important. It was a measure of how well things were going for you when you were sixteen, but it was funny for me to hear Angie and I talk about it in that way. I was a long way from getting a car, and I was talking to her like it was about to happen. I needed to change the subject.

"I'll just be glad if I can get this job and make some money. It'll be something different from working in the store all the time," I told her.

"I think about doing different things," she said immediately. "I mean the drugstore is okay, but it gets kind of boring sometimes. I don't know what else I could do, but maybe something."

"You're just starting," I answered. "You've got time to do other things."

"I could never be on the radio," she said. "How many girls are there on the radio?"

I hadn't really thought about it, but when she said it I couldn't think of any.

"The radio or the television," she continued. "It's all men. What if I wanted to be on the radio, or the television?"

"I don't know Angie. I don't even know how to be on the radio yet," I answered.

"Well, when you do get on the radio maybe you can think about it. You can think about how to get girls on the radio too. That seems fair."

"I guess, but like I said there's not much I can do about it," I said, kind of exasperated. We sat quietly until Angie pulled her car in behind the drugstore.

"Thanks for the ride," I said, and smiled at her.

"You're welcome anytime Neil. I come up here most days after school. If you need a ride you can let me know," she said. She caught me off guard again, and I just said "okay." I should have said "great" or something like that, but I didn't. Now I would have to think about why I didn't say that.

She went in to work, and I walked over to Craig's Appliance store to find a radio. I picked out a little RCA transistor radio with an earpiece and a hand-strap. There were some very nice stereo receivers in the store that I would have loved to buy. I thought about the money I might be making soon and added a stereo to the list of things I wanted to get— the list that began with a car.

I had about a dollar leftover, so I went back over to the drugstore to buy a drink and hopefully talk to Angie some more. She was at the back register when I came in, so I sat up at the soda fountain and waited. I was fiddling with my new radio when Ben walked up from the back of the store and sat down beside me.

"New radio?" he asked. I felt a little silly holding the thing. Transistor radios were kind of dinky. Ben had a stereo receiver in his room, and he had a radio in his car. I was nearly sixteen-years-old, and I was showing off a nine-dollar toy radio with a strap on it.

"Yeah, I got it for work," I told him.

"You're going to use that at work?"

"Well, not really at work. I'm going to use it to get ready to work," I tried to explain. "I'm supposed to listen to WHJ. It's easy to carry."

Angie walked up to the soda fountain, smiling, and said hello.

"Have you seen Neil's new piece of radio equipment?" Ben said to her, pointing towards my little radio.

"Asshole," I said quietly to him so no one else in the store could hear. He was just messing with me and Angie knew it.

"Ben wouldn't even know how to work that," she said, "much less a whole radio station."

Ben laughed. "Angie, that's mean. You hurt my

feelings."

"You don't have a whole lot of feelings to hurt," she shot back.

"I've got to get going. See you tonight," Ben said to me.

"Yeah, tonight."

Angie wanted to know what we were doing. I told her we were getting together to work on Algebra. I didn't tell her that I was the one who needed help, but she knew Ben didn't need help from me. He was one of the best in class.

I ordered a cherry-limeade, and Angie and I talked for a pretty long time. We talked about teachers, about friends, about music—whatever came to mind. It was nice. I looked at her and imagined us on a date, spending time together and talking like this. I didn't really know much about dating. I had only been on a few dates, all of them to dances. But just two people, with no other kids around, doing whatever came to mind would be a lot different. I tried not to distract myself too much thinking about it while we were talking. Time passed quickly, and I needed to get to work myself. I told Angie I had to go, and she said, "good luck with the Algebra." The way she said it made me feel better. I said thanks and left for home, wondering again if I could have said more.

I turned on my little radio and slipped the earpiece in. I turned the thing on and tuned it down to WHJ at just past the number thirteen on the dial. They were playing a song called "Lean on Me" that I had heard before on a Memphis station. The song ended and a guy came on the radio talking loudly about the song and about the "Big Thirteen". I recognized the voice. It was Chris, one of the seniors from the high school who would be leaving the station soon. He played some commercials. I recognized those voices too. It was Woody and then Bobby talking about a grocery store and about Craig's Appliance Center, the place where I bought my radio. The commercials played and then a bunch of singers came on singing WHJ. Another song started and Chris was talking again. "Sunny and eighty-four degrees at five-seventeen. I'm Chris Sanders and this is the Big 13, WHJ with Gallery, and "It's So Nice To Be With You," and that's true."

I listened and pictured Chris sitting in the control room working the board. It made me anxious to picture myself in his place. I wanted to get as comfortable as possible before going on the radio. It was hard to imagine, but as I listened I was trying to get more used to the idea that this might happen. I needed to get on with it.

I got to the store a little before six and helped my mother until we closed. We went home, and I waited for Ben to come by and give me a ride. He pulled in front of our house a little later in his father's old Mustang. It was hard not to be jealous of the car. It looked great, and it was the kind of car most of us could only dream about. Ben never acted too proud driving it, and he was always willing to give someone a ride. We were jealous for sure, but it was better because it was Ben.

"What's up Mr. DJ," Ben said, first thing.

"Yeah, I don't know about all that," I answered.

"Well, I do. It's going to happen, Neil," he said to me in a way that gave me a little shot of confidence. Ben was good at that. He liked to kid around, but he could also pick out moments and say things that could make you feel better. People liked him for that. He had only lived in Harper's Junction for three years, and he was one of the most popular kids in our class.

We pulled into Ben's house, and he and I stood out in his driveway and talked until Coy got there. You couldn't miss Coy in the old truck he drove. It was older than he was, and it was neat to see him fuss over it like he did. I know it made him feel a little better about losing his grandfather. They had been very close. I heard the truck before I saw it. It made a unique sound, the sound only a twenty-something-year-old truck could make. Coy pulled up beside us, flung open the door, and bounced down from the seat.

"You boys ready for some Al-gee-bra?" he said, trying to sound funny.

The three of us were standing outside, in no rush to get to work, when Ben's daddy pulled in and parked his car behind the house.

"Hey boys." He had seen Ben and Coy just minutes ago at the drugstore, so he called me by name. "Neil, how are you doing?"

"Fine sir," I answered.

"Ben told me about the job at the radio station. That's very exciting, could be a really good experience for you."

"I hope so," I said. "I haven't really gotten it all worked out yet. I've got to learn how to do it first."

"You'll do fine. Keep a good attitude and learn all you can, and it'll go all right," he said.

"I'll try to," I said, smiling. I really appreciated him saying what he did. It sounded to me like something a father should say, but mine never did, and never would.

"What are you boys doing tonight?" he asked the three of us.

"Algebra," Ben answered.

"Sounds like fun," he said and walked towards the

house. "Good luck."

"Yeah, fun," Coy repeated sarcastically.

We all went inside. Ben's mother was sitting on the couch watching *The Flip Wilson Show*. Flip was doing Geraldine. He was dressed like a woman, in a mini-skirt and go-go boots, and he was flirting with Jim Brown. She said hello to Coy and me and told us to help ourselves to something to eat and drink, before going back to watching the television show. Ben led us into the kitchen, and we got cokes and chips to take back to his room. Ben turned on his stereo receiver and stacked a couple of albums up for us to listen to while we worked.

I looked at the covers of the albums he had chosen. One was "Eat a Peach" by the Allman Brothers and the other was "Jackson Browne" by Jackson Browne. I barely knew the Allman Brothers, and I had never heard of Jackson Browne. It seemed like Ben was always ahead of us with music, and a lot of other things too. He had moved to Harper's Junction from Chicago when he was thirteen-years-old. His father had bought a drugstore on the square and moved down here in the summer of 1968. Ben stood out from the rest of us, but at the same time he was able to blend in. He had been more places and seen more things than I could imagine.

The music was great, but it didn't help much with the Algebra. Ben worked through a couple of problems, and I kind of pretended I knew what was going on. He sensed that and went back over the same problems for my benefit. I finally made a little progress and began to feel slightly better about the situation. Coy was learning too, and Ben seemed pleased that he was helping us. He also never seemed annoyed by having to help us. I really appreciated that, but I didn't tell him. We gave up on the Algebra and began just listening to the music. I made the mistake of saying something about Angie. Coy picked up on it right away and began singing the Rolling Stones song by the same title.

"You suck," I said, trying to stop the singing.

"Yeah, really bad," Ben added. "Please don't sing, because you can't sing."

"That's your opinion. I like the way I sound," Coy said.

"That would be you and no one else," I said.

"I can't believe you even like the way you sound," Ben said, with a smile.

I was hoping they had been distracted from talking about Angie, but they hadn't.

"Does look like someone has an eye for Angie," Ben said.

"I didn't say that," I answered.

"Didn't have to," Coy added, and started singing again. "Angie, you're beautiful…"

"That's not any better," I said.

"So, how about it," Ben asked. "You gonna ask Angie out?"

"Hadn't really thought about it," I said.

Ben smiled. "I think you have thought about it."

Of course, I had thought about it, but I figured I shouldn't admit it here. They worked with Angie, and I didn't want them saying anything to her about it.

"Why would I tell you if I had thought about it?" I told Ben.

"Don't have to," he said. "She might go out with you."

"I just said…"

"I heard what you just said. Where would you take her? You know she's dated some older boys. You would have to come up with something pretty special."

"When's the last time you had a date?" I asked.

"Got you there," Coy said. "I'm pretty sure he's O for 1972."

Ben laughed. "Well, that's my choice. I have chosen not to date lately."

"Your choice, my butt," Coy said. "Let me know when you're about to 'choose' to ask a girl out. I want to see that."

"I'm not going to ask just anyone out," Ben said.

"That's it," Coy answered. "You're not going to ask just anyone, or anyone else out."

It went on like that. We were having a good time, kidding each other and listening to Ben's albums. It got late, and I was hoping to get home before my father did. It might not matter if I was out too late, but I never knew from one day to the next what would set him off. And he might not be home yet, or he could have gotten home and gone straight to bed. The thing I feared was the possibility that he had gotten home, but hadn't gone to sleep. I didn't want to see him. I never wanted to see him, especially late at night.

Coy drove me home. I sat thinking about how to ask Angie out and trying not to think too much about what I might face at home. His truck was there. My father was home, and my first impulse was to tell Coy to back out of the driveway and find someplace else to go. I couldn't do that, so I sat there for a few moments and tried to calm myself before going inside. I could see that the back bedroom light was off, and I hoped that meant he had gone to bed and that would be the end of it for the night.

My mother was sitting on the couch with the lights off, smoking a cigarette, when I walked in the living room. She made a schussing gesture and nodded towards the back of the house. That meant he was in bed, and I should be quiet getting to my bedroom. I practically tiptoed down the hall, pushed my bedroom door open very slowly, and stepped inside. I closed the door behind me even more carefully than I had opened it and cringed when it made a slight creaking sound. I was tempted to get under the covers with my clothes on. It would be quicker and less noisy, and I would have clothes on if I needed to run. Instead, I slipped off my pants and shirt and got in bed. I don't know how long, but it took me a long time to fall asleep. I thought about the radio station and the job. And as much as it surprised me to be in this situation, I knew I should try to take advantage of it.

Chapter 4

I got a ride from Coy after school Friday. He had the windows rolled down and looked happy behind the wheel. He dropped me off at the store. My mother was behind the counter and my grandmother was right alongside her. I went straight to the telephone and called WHJ.

Louise Burns answered the phone, and not in a friendly way. WHJ was all she said and she seemed annoyed at having to answer.

"This is Neil Robinson. Is Woody there?"

"No he is not," she answered.

I tried to sound business-like. "Do you expect him back," I asked.

'It's Friday afternoon. No, I don't," she answered.

"I was going to tell him that I would be coming up to the radio station this weekend," I told her.

"I'll leave the boys a note, and they will know to expect you," she answered. I was surprised that she took care of things so quickly. I didn't expect her to help.

"Well, thank you Mrs. Burns," I told her.

"You're welcome, Mr. Robinson," she answered with a bit of a smile in her voice.

My mother and grandmother heard enough of the conversation to know what I was doing. "You're starting this weekend?" my mother asked.

"I guess so. I figured I would go up there for a little while tomorrow.

She seemed pleased. "I think that's a good idea," she said. My grandmother smiled too. Everyone was acting like this was a big thing.

I got to the radio station at about eight o'clock on Saturday morning. I had walked to the square with my little radio in hand and my earpiece in. Chris was working, and I had heard him announce several songs, along with an announcement about summer baseball sign-ups in Harper's Junction. I was standing at the top of the stairs about to flip the secret switch when I heard him on the radio saying "This is 1330, WHJ, Harper's Junction Tennessee! It's eight o'clock." The news came on in another person's voice, so I reached up and flipped the switch a couple of times and waited. Less than a minute later the door to the station opened.

"Come on in," he said. "I got a note from Louise about you coming up."

"Yeah, is it alright?" I asked, wanting to be sure.

"Sure," he said and walked quickly back to the control room. "Pull that chair in here," he said, pointing to the chair in the production room. I rolled it into the control room and placed it in the small space behind where the announcer sat.

"Here?" I asked Chris.

"Sure," he answered again and sat down.

I sat down behind him, watching and waiting for the next thing. Chris slapped a couple of tape cartridges into the tape players to his right, pulled his headphones up from around his neck and placed them over his ears. He glanced out the window and then up at the clock in front of him, before turning on the microphone switch at the far end of the board. When he did, the room went quiet. There was nothing coming through the speakers that were mounted high on both sides of the small room. We sat there a few seconds before Chris broke the silence.

"Sunny and seventy-two degrees in Harper's Junction," he said with enthusiasm, and then hit a green button on the tape player nearest to him. He was quiet again for just a couple of seconds before hitting the green button on the second machine and launching into: "WHJ with something for this sunny Saturday morning. John Denver has got it right. Sunshine on your shoulders sure can make you happy!" He pulled off the headphones and turned around to look at me. I grinned and nodded at him. I thought that was good, what he said. He didn't smile back.

"So you want to do this?" he asked.

"I think so," I answered. "You like it?" I expected him to answer yes, but that's not what he said.

"It's okay, I guess, but I'm ready to get out of here." That surprised me.

"Why is that?"

"It was fun for a while…I don't know. I'm ready to go on to college. I guess it's Harper's Junction and high school. It's just time to go," he explained.

I was just ending my sophomore year, and I was expecting, or maybe just hoping, the next two years would be better—more fun anyway. Now this guy was saying that he was glad it was over.

"Where are you going to college? I asked.

"Hang on," he said, turning around to face the microphone again. He slipped the headphones on, grabbed the switch on the far left of the board again, and glanced up at the clock.

"A little happier now?" he said into the microphone. "I'm Chris Sanders and this is 1330 WHJ at thirteen minutes past eight o'clock. Here's that late sleeper Cat Stevens with

'Morning Has Broken,' on WHJ." I was grinning again when Chris turned around. He was good at this. Still, I got no reaction from him.

"Memphis State," he said, answering my question from before. I was impressed by how quickly he could turn on the radio personality and then turn it off again.

"Oh, that should be good," I said, not really knowing much about Memphis State.

"I think it will be okay. I'm looking forward to Memphis anyway."

"Are you going to work on the radio there?" I asked.

"I've thought about it. Maybe, if I need a job, but I'd like to just be in college–go to school and do all that," he explained.

I imagined that doing radio in Memphis would be as much fun as going to college there, maybe more, but I didn't say it. I was trying to get excited about working at WHJ, and Chris seemed like he was over whatever might have made him happy about being on the radio.

"I'm just ready for something else," he said, sounding more tired than I would have ever expected from an eighteen-year-old in his position. I thought about trying to draw him out a little and see if he would talk about how he felt when he first started working at the station. I didn't try though. For now, what I knew was that almost everyone around me thought this would be a good job, but the guy doing the job didn't sound like it. At least he didn't sound that way early on a Saturday morning talking to me, but for people listening to him on the radio, they would have never guessed that he felt that way.

Chris turned back to face the microphone again, and I realized after watching him for only a few minutes that things happened very quickly in the control room. He was changing out tapes and looking at the long sheets of paper in front of him every couple of minutes. The songs were short, and he had to be ready with something else when the songs ended. He started another song and then stacked up several carts to play when that song was over. It was a stack of recorded commercials that he moved in and out of the tape players. After playing several commercials, he played a recording of some people singing "The Big 13," WHJ and got back into another song.

"This all happens pretty fast in here," I said to him when he finished introducing the song.

"I know it seems that way," he said. "That's what I thought at first, but you get used to it, and things will slow down for you. It's not that complicated. What matters is how you sound and what you say. That's the stuff you'll have to work on the most. Almost anybody can run the board," he said. It was pretty much the same thing that Woody had said to me. Still, I was most worried right now with learning what the buttons and switches did. I could worry about what to say later.

"If you have questions, just ask," Chris said.

"Thanks, I appreciate that," I answered

We didn't talk much after that. I sat and watched him work. He kept things going smoothly, and he seemed very comfortable doing it. He had been working at the station for a couple of years, and I had to wonder if he knew as little as I did when he started.

"How did you get this job?" I asked Chris after watching him for over an hour.

"Oh, I don't know. I guess my Daddy knows Woody, and maybe he said something to him about it. I liked the radio a lot growing up, but I never thought about trying to do it."

"How long did it take for you to learn all this?" I asked him.

"It didn't take that long," he told me. "It shouldn't take you that long either. Like I said, work on what you sound like and what you're gonna say. You don't want to sound stupid."

No, I didn't want to sound stupid. That's for sure. I hadn't thought much about sounding stupid until now. Bad, yes. Stupid was a new worry.

Two hours seemed like long enough to stay. I didn't want to annoy Chris since I was going to need his help the next few weeks. I told him thanks and left the station. I looked across the square at Geist's Drug Store and headed there, hoping that Angie was working. I was disappointed to see Coy behind the soda fountain when I looked in the store window.

"She's not here," he said to me, first thing. I tried to act innocent.

"Who?"

"Who you're looking for, that's who," he said. I didn't respond.

"You working all day?" I asked, trying to change the subject.

"She'll be here later," he said.

"Okay. What's Ben doing?"

"He's off. She's working noon till close," Coy answered.

"Okay. Are y'all doing anything tonight?" I asked.

"We haven't talked about it. We might hang out. You want me to come get you, or will Angie pick you up?"

"Not funny."

Coy laughed, "See you tonight then."

I left the drugstore and turned down the street towards

our store. I pulled out my little radio, turned it on, and put the earphone in. A song was ending and Chris was on the air. "Sweet, Sweet Seasons on My Mind. That's Carol King and I'm Chris Sanders with nothing but a sweet weekend on my mind." The singers burst out again with WHJ and the next song was on. I pictured the buttons being pushed and the switches being flipped as his show continued. Chris was still driving things forward, and he had been on the radio since early in the day. I hadn't thought about it before, but he was using a lot of energy and I didn't know how long he would work on the radio today. This was another hint that doing radio won't be easy, at least not as easy as he made it sound.

I got to the store and started to work. My mother needed to take my little sister to a friend's house, so she left me to handle our little grocery store alone for a while. Our store never got real busy; Robinson's Grocery was a place where people who lived close by would buy a few things. Not many people bought all their groceries from us.

My mother had opened the store with the help of my grandfather when things started to get bad at home. My father stayed away a lot and spent a lot of the money he made on things other than our family. We needed help, and my grandfather had stepped up to help us. It put more strain on my mother, but it also helped us get by. Me taking a job at the radio station would be an added strain for her since I wouldn't be around to help as much. My father came by the store occasionally, though he seldom stuck around to help, so I was a little surprised—but mostly unhappy—to see him pull up in his truck while I was working alone.

He walked in and opened the cash register first thing. He looked in the cash drawer and pulled out some money. I couldn't see what he took, and of course I didn't say anything. I had seen him do this plenty of times before, and it made my mother madder than anything for him to breeze through our store and take money she had been working all day to make.

He stuffed the money in his pocket and looked straight at me.

"You know you're going to have to keep helping your momma," he said, without explaining what he meant. I knew it meant he had heard about the radio job, and he was telling me what he didn't like about the idea. I didn't answer.

"You just can't run out of here and do anything you damn well please," he added. No questions about the job, no congratulations, no nothing but anger from him. I said nothing, and he left to go do what he damn well pleased, I guess.

Momma came back and we closed the store. She counted the money and looked over to me. I knew what she was about to say.

"Has your daddy been here?

"Yeah," was all I said.

"He got in the cash register?" she wanted to know.

"Yeah."

"Figures. I can't believe him," she said, shaking her head.

I started to tell her what he said to me, but decided against it. It wouldn't help anything, and she was upset enough about the money he took.

"I'm meeting Coy. We're going to hang out."

"Don't be out too late," she said. "Be home before your daddy."

I didn't answer. Neither of us knew when that might be. It might be midnight, daylight, or even tomorrow night, before he came home.

I walked over to the house and waited out back for Coy to come by. I was glad to see him pull his granddaddy's truck into our driveway.

"I told Ben we would meet him at Sam's," Coy said as I climbed in.

We drove up to the square and turned down Washington Street out towards the highway and Sam's. We passed The Dairy Queen along the way and saw the kids hanging out there. Saturday night meant cruising in Harper's Junction. We drove our cars around town—mostly in a loop between a burger joint called Sam's Drive-In and the Dairy Queen. After a few loops, we parked at one place or the other, at least until we figured it was time to cruise some more and maybe park at the other place. Kids without cars rode with other kids, and there was a lot of swapping from one car to another. At some point most every Saturday night, we figured out that nothing different or exciting was going to happen, but it was pretty much all that we had. I kept an eye out for Angie's car. There was a chance she would be out after getting off work.

We pulled off the highway and made a loop around Sam's. We saw Ben's Mustang, and Coy pulled his truck in alongside it. Ben was out talking to some of our friends. Coy let the tailgate down on his truck, and he and I took a seat there. We sat and watched the stream of cars moving in a circle around Sam's. A few kids stopped their cars and joined us, most just waved and kept going.

I sat on the tailgate and replayed what had happened to me today. I was trying to figure out Chris' attitude about his job at the radio station. He had surprised me. I guess I understood some of his feelings about getting out of Harper's Junction. I didn't know him very well, so I wondered if there were reasons that he felt the way he did. That led me to think about my father. I wasn't surprised by his reaction to seeing me today and by what he said, but as always it hurt my feelings, and it made me sad. I was always going back and forth between anger and sadness with him.

The cars rolled by, and I kept watching for Angie's blue Chevrolet. I knew I was getting way ahead of myself in thinking about her, but she seemed more interested in me since hearing about the radio thing. I wondered if that was a good reason for her to be interested in me, but I really didn't care much either. Whatever reason she might have was enough.

I kept watching, but she never came around. Ben, Coy, and I sat and talked while the same cars and the same people came around the place time after time. We enjoyed each other's company, and it was good to be out on a warm night. Though without saying it, we were hoping that something out of the ordinary would happen. Nothing did. And just like a lot of Saturday nights for teenagers in Harper's Junction, that's the way the night ended for us.

Chapter 5

"His truck ran off Old River Bridge and he drowned." That's what I heard the Sheriff tell my momma. I was in bed, trying not to hear what he was saying. He didn't have to explain. I knew Daddy was drunk and ran off a bridge. I had prayed for him to die, and now this man was saying that my prayer had been answered.

I was frozen to the bed. I should have gotten up and gone to be with my mother, but I couldn't get up. I needed time to think about how I should react. I knew I shouldn't seem relieved, but I think I was. I didn't have to face him anymore. That's what I knew. I wouldn't have to pray for the strength to kill him either. That strength never came anyway. If it had come, he would have been dead before now.

I couldn't hear my mother saying anything to the Sheriff. Maybe she wasn't able to speak, or maybe she didn't want to say what came to her mind.

"Lois, if there is anything you need, if there is anything I can help you with, you call me. Okay?" the Sheriff told her. "We'll be praying for you and your family." Again, I heard nothing from Momma.

I stayed in bed and imagined her sitting on the couch, quietly smoking a cigarette, and not knowing what to do next. My little sister was sleeping in her room, and I was pretty sure she hadn't heard what had been said. She would have gotten up if she had. Ginny slept through a lot of the things that happened in our house late at night with my father. She could have heard some of it, but I don't think she had heard the worst of it. Now my mother would have to tell Ginny that Daddy was dead, and I knew it would be very hard for both of them.

I let the time pass and let my mind wander. I tried to remember what had happened to other kids who had had a parent die. There weren't many. I knew there would be a big fuss though, and I would get a lot of attention that I didn't want. I had never told anyone about my father and the prayers, and I didn't think that anyone knew how bad things were. Ben and Coy knew a little, but not nearly all of it. They knew he wasn't around a lot, but I don't think they suspected that we were all afraid of him, all the time.

There was no noise from my mother. I began to worry about her and decided to get up and go face her. I sat on the side of the bed and stared at my bedroom door. I knew that once I went out into the living room and saw her this would start to become real. I left my room and turned down the hall into the living room. She was sitting at the end of the couch, staring out the window. I stopped and looked at her for what felt like a long time before she took notice of me. She must have seen in the look on my face that I knew.

"He's gone, and we're going to be alright, Neil," is what she said to me. I sat down in the chair next to the couch and nothing else was said. I watched her as she continued to look out on to the street in front of our house. The sun was coming through from the left and it streaked across her face. I couldn't tell if she was happy or sad. She just looked empty, mostly.

I didn't hear Ginny get up. She appeared, standing at the end of the hallway in her pajamas, looking at the two of us. My mother looked over at her and then at me. She sighed, took a deep breath, and motioned Ginny over to sit next to her. Momma put her arm around her and pulled her in close. Ginny looked up at her, puzzled.

"Ginny, something terrible has happened," she started saying. "It's your daddy, he's been in a car wreck. I'm sorry sweetheart. He didn't make it," she said, and paused.

"What do you mean he didn't make it?" Ginny said, repeating Momma's words.

"He didn't make it sweetheart. Your daddy died in a car wreck last night." Momma grimaced like she couldn't get any more words to come out. Ginny stared at Momma's face trying to make sense out of what she had just heard. Then she looked at me as if I could make her understand what was happening, but I had no words for her.

"No," was the first thing Ginny said. She kept saying it until it built into a scream. "No, No, No, No! No! No! No!! My Daddy did not die in a car wreck," she screamed. "My daddy is not dead!"

She jerked away from my mother and ran down the hall to look for him in their bedroom. Not seeing him there, she turned and ran for the back door and looked out into the driveway.

"No! No! No!" She was hysterical. I got up and walked toward her.

"Don't touch me!" she screamed several times and ran out the door. My mother nodded at me as if to signal for me to go after her, and I did. I chased her through the yard and into the trees behind our house. She ran away from me as fast as she could before collapsing under a big maple tree.

She was crying so hard that she was having trouble catching her breath. I stood quietly beside her, hoping to not make things worse. She looked up at me through her tears with a puzzled look, and I realized that I was not crying, and maybe she was wondering why not. Either way, I did wonder about my reaction.

"Let's go in the house," I finally said to her.

"I can't go in there," she answered, sobbing.

"Please, Momma needs us," I said. "She needs you."

"I need my daddy! Tell me it's not true," she screamed back at me. There was nothing I could say. I tried to help her up, but she fell back down several times before she could stand. I held her arm, and we walked slowly back to the house. Ginny stopped several times along the way and bent over like she was going to faint.

Momma was standing at the back door when we finally made it out of the trees and into the yard. She rushed out to grab Ginny who went limp when Momma put her arm around her.

"Baby, I'm so sorry," Momma said to her. "I'm so sorry." Momma looked over at me. And, like me, she wasn't crying. "Let's go inside," she said to the both of us. Momma sat Ginny down beside her on the couch and put her arm around her. Ginny sobbed

I left the two of them sitting there and went to my bedroom to lie down. There was a lot about what I had just heard and seen that didn't seem one bit real. It was one of those times when I believed it was possible that I might just wake up from all of this—that it might really be just a dream, but I had thought about something like this happening to him for as long as I could remember. Ginny was only twelve-years-old and for whatever reasons, daddy had been more careful about the way he treated her. She knew how he was, but I'm sure she never pictured him running off a bridge and dying in a car wreck. I had.

I wondered what would happen next—what we would have to go through to try and get past this thing that I had only learned about a couple of hours ago. I already wanted that part of it to be over, but it was just starting. I reached over and took my little radio off the table beside my bed and put the earplug in. I turned on my favorite station out of Memphis and let the songs roll through my head. And despite the uncertainty of the moment, I felt tension leaving my head and my body. I was relaxed, and I knew why

Chapter 6

I didn't go to school that week. I didn't do much of anything really. There was a lot of sitting around. We sat at the house and people came by. We sat at the funeral home and people came by there to see us. We sat through the funeral, and later, we came home and sat around the house again. People were nice to us. Some of them seemed to know what to say, like they were saying things that they had said before. Other people didn't know what to say, most just said how sorry they were.

A lot of people brought food. My grandmother was with us for most of the week. She talked to people who came by to see us, and she organized the food. My mother didn't say much and didn't eat much. Nana kept reminding her to eat, and she wouldn't. A lot of the people who came by said they would pray for us. Many of them said that if there was anything they could do for us, to let them know. Momma had no response for them, and neither did I. I couldn't imagine what they could do for her or me. I almost laughed at one of them when it crossed my mind that I needed someone to do my Algebra for me.

A preacher came by our house every day that week. We weren't church people. We didn't go to church. Because of my father, we didn't do much of anything as a family. My mother had attended church as a child, and this preacher was the new minister there. They didn't know each other except by name. He would sit and talk to my mother, and she wouldn't react. She barely said anything to him. The preacher told Nana that he thought my mother was in shock, and that she should watch her closely.

She wasn't talking, and I guessed in part that was because she didn't want to tell people what she was thinking. They were going on and on about how terrible this all was for her and our family, calling her "you poor thing" and such. There was no way I could know or understand all of her feelings, but I think I got it a little. She had been married to Daddy for nearly twenty years, and he was the father of her children. And despite all that, right now, I believe she was relieved that she didn't have to deal with him anymore.

Daddy's sister, my Aunt Bobby, caused the most trouble the week of the funeral. She knew more than anyone outside of the three of us about my father's problems, and she liked to blame his problems on my mother. They couldn't stand each other. She came in the house the afternoon daddy died with a mixture of anger and tears.

"I knew this was going to happen," she started. "My brother, my big brother," she was crying loudly. "Someone should have taken care of him. Why didn't someone take care of him," she said in the direction of my mother. Momma didn't say a thing. "These poor children. Their daddy is gone, and I can't do a thing about it. My brother tried so hard to please you, and he never could," she said. "You should have been better to him. That's why he drank." That's when my grandmother spoke up from out in the kitchen.

"That's enough Bobby. You don't talk to her like that. You know better." Nana stepped in the living room and stood between Momma and Aunt Bobby. "If you can't act any better than this, you need to go home and leave us alone."

"You old bitch," Bobby yelled at Nana. "You're the reason she's the way she is."

"Leave now," Nana said in way that shut Bobby up

for a second. She turned like she was leaving, but stopped to look at me.

"Neil if you need a place to stay, you can always come and stay with Carl and me," she said. My mother finally spoke up.

"Get out of my house!" she yelled at Bobby, who then marched out through the front door and left. I expected the exchange to break my mother a little, but her expression didn't change. She reached over, pulled a cigarette out of a pack, and lit it. I was stunned by what I heard from my aunt, my grandmother, and mother. I guess I didn't fully realize how bad it was between Momma and Daddy's sister until that moment.

We all went down the funeral home the next night. Ginny and Nana sat with Momma in a room near the casket and talked to people as they came through. My Uncle Ray came up from Memphis and sat with her for most of the time too. It seemed to help. Momma was able to talk to him a little. She still didn't have much to say to the others. Aunt Bobby and her family were there, but they didn't come near my mother. She stood near my father's casket, which thankfully was closed, for most of the evening. I was sitting as far away from them, and from Daddy's body, as I could.

I found some chairs set up in the corner of a mostly empty room, and I was sitting by myself when Ben, Coy, and Angie came walking towards me. I hadn't thought about the possibility of my friends coming by the funeral home. I felt a catch in my throat. I still hadn't cried, but seeing them, and realizing that they were there for me, made my eyes water. I tried to stop myself from a big cry.

Angie sat right down beside me and put her arm around me. She smiled and put her head on my shoulder for a second. Ben and Coy stood in front of us and fumbled around trying to put their hands in their pockets.

"Sit down," Angie said to them quietly, and they did.

Angie did all the talking. She asked me if I was okay and if my mother and Ginny were okay. Ben and Coy were having trouble looking me in the eye. I wouldn't have a clue about what to say if one of their fathers had been killed. We all sat quietly for what seemed like a long time, before Angie tried to change the subject for a moment.

"Are you going back to the radio station this week?" she asked me.

"I think I will. I think I want to," I said.

"That's good," she said. "It'll give you something to work on, to think about."

"Yeah, I believe you're right," I said. "We've got finals next week too."

Ben spoke up. "I'll help you with that, anything you need," he said and smiled a little. I was glad that he said it, and I think it was a relief to him to be able to offer something to me that might really help.

Uncle Ray brought one of my cousins over to say hello to me. Another couple of family members that I never saw and barely knew followed them over. I wanted to sit quietly with my friends, but now I was being dragged into a line of people who wanted to tell me how sorry they were. I was sorry too, that we had to do all this. Angie caught my attention and motioned to me that they were leaving. I should have gone over to her and said how much I appreciated them coming, but I couldn't get to them.

The night dragged on past the time that we had planned on leaving. I watched my mother and sister closely from a distance. Ginny was tearing up every time another person came by to speak with her. My mother was mostly expressionless. She nodded occasionally and said a few words when she had to, but mostly she kept quiet, and she seemed in control of herself. I was relieved when the people all cleared out, and it looked like we were going to get to leave. I had the urge to go to Ben's house, or Coy's, or cruise around town on the chance that the three of them were still together, and I would see Angie.

Instead, Nana, Momma, Ginny, and I were still here, along with Aunt Bobby, who was still standing by the casket. It seemed like we were waiting on something, but I couldn't imagine what it was, and I didn't ask. A short time later, the funeral home director walked past us and stood beside Bobby. They spoke in whispers for a few moments, before he walked up to the casket and raised the lid. With that, he closed the doors to the room we were sitting in and disappeared. I didn't know what was going on. Momma and Nana didn't seem surprised.

I hadn't asked why his casket had been closed. I didn't want to know why, and I did not want it open. I had seen the bodies of my grandparents lying in caskets. It was creepy, but they looked mostly peaceful and harmless. I didn't want to see my father's body for any reason. I was scared of it, just like I was scared of him. It would have suited me if his casket was nailed shut with him in it, maybe that way I wouldn't have to dream of him raising up and getting his hands on us. But it was open, and from where I was sitting I could see a nose, a little bit of a face, and his hands folded across his chest. Aunt Bobby moved in close by the casket and began wailing. She was patting his hands.

"My sweet, sweet brother," she cried loudly. "What have they done to you? You were such a pretty boy. Momma loved you so, so much. Now you're all gone, and I am here by myself. What will I do without you?"

She sounded like she was making a speech—a phony speech. My mother wouldn't look at her or the casket. Ginny was sitting up in her chair, nearly standing to try and get a better look. She forced herself up from the chair and took a step or two towards the casket. Momma motioned at me to go with her. I wasn't sure if my legs would work. I felt stuck to the chair, unable or unwilling to move toward my father's body. Ginny took a couple of more steps, and I was able to push myself up off the chair and move slowly toward her. I was supposed to be helping her in some way, but I stayed behind Ginny as she moved closer to the body, hoping that she would offer me some protection.

We got close enough to the casket to see his full face and Ginny began to scream. I would have screamed too, if I could have gotten a sound to come out. The thing in the casket barely looked like our Daddy. There was a line of thick, black stitches across his forehead. Another line of stitches cut across his face, through his lips and down his chin. He had been torn apart in a wreck and sewn back together to lie in this casket. He looked like Frankenstein, and that was why the casket had been closed all night. Opening it now for my little sister to see was a terrible idea.

Aunt Bobby started to put her arm around Ginny. "Your daddy loved you so much," she said. Bobby was making things worse, and I didn't know what to do. My mother wasn't moving. Nana got up and walked towards Ginny. Ginny saw her and pulled away from Bobby.

"That's enough," Nana said, and glared at my aunt. Nana got me by the arm too. "Let's go home," she said, and led the two of us toward the door. "Come on Lois," she said to my mother. Momma got up slowly and turned like she was leaving with us, but she stopped and glared back at Bobby, who huffed and walked out without saying anything else. Momma paused for a few moments, then turned and stepped up beside daddy's casket. She looked over his disfigured face for just a few seconds, shook her head a couple of times, and walked out with us. She didn't cry.

The funeral was a blur. It was hard to distinguish between what was actually said and what was only in my head. I was lost in my own thoughts as I tried to get through the day without thinking too much about what was being said to me by these people who came to the funeral, and about what was said during the funeral service by a preacher who knew nothing about my father. I was sure the two of them had never met.

The preacher mentioned us—Momma, Ginny and me, along with Aunt Bobby, and he talked a little about my father's service in the army during World War II. Mostly he talked about eternity and the things we all needed to do before we faced god. He never said my father had done those things, and it was almost a sure thing that he hadn't. We all had time to take care of those things, he said, but we needed to act now. We could all see by the man in the casket in front of us that we might not have that chance tomorrow. Tomorrow was not guaranteed to any of us, he said.

He talked on for some time, and I stopped listening. I looked around the chapel at the people at the service. Some of them were childhood friends of my mother, people who still lived in Harper's Junction that my mother rarely saw anymore.

There were a few people my father had known growing up too. They came from a community a few miles over.

My father moved to Harper's Junction after serving in the army. My mother was barely eighteen-years-old and still in high school when they met. He was a twenty-five-year-old veteran who had served in the Pacific, and he impressed my mother with his worldliness and looks. They married quickly without knowing much of anything about each other. And it seemed to me that what they learned since then was that they couldn't get along. I knew that Daddy's drinking caused a lot of their problems now, but I didn't know which came first— the drinking or the problems that might have come before the drinking. I couldn't imagine blaming my mother for any of it, but he sure did.

The preacher finally called for a prayer to end the service, and I was struck with the thought that I had nothing to pray for anymore. I had been praying for the strength to kill my father, or that he would die in some other way so that none of us had to face him anymore. Now it was done, and I wondered what, if anything, I would see fit to pray for next.

The prayer ended, and the people in the chapel filed out, most of them pausing by the casket. Some bowed their heads for a moment, others nodded, and a few touched the casket. We sat and waited for them all to leave. The preacher was the last one out. Momma, Nana, Ginny, Aunt Bobby, and I were the only ones left. The funeral director moved quietly into the room and walked to the casket. It looked like he was about to open the casket lid, just as he had the night before. He paused and nodded at my mother, as if he was asking her for permission to open it.

My mother, who hadn't made a sound above a whisper

in three days, screamed "No, no, no! Do not open that thing!"

The man was startled and backed away from the casket. "Yes ma'am, of course," he said to her, and started to leave. Aunt Bobby tried to stop him.

"Open that casket," she ordered. "I want to see my brother right now. If you won't do it, I will," she yelled.

"Bobby, you and Lois will need to work this out," he said, in almost a whisper, and left. Bobby glared at my mother who spoke up again.

"No, we're done," she said. "Leave him and the casket alone. We're done," she repeated.

"That's my brother," Bobby yelled.

"Yeah, and he's my husband and their daddy, and I'm telling you leave it alone," Momma said.

"You'll pay for this," Bobby said, sounding like she was speaking to the four of us.

"We've already paid for it," my mother answered.

Bobby left. She couldn't have been madder. I was shocked by the exchange. My mother had always tolerated Aunt Bobby pretty well, but it sounded like things had changed. The man from the funeral home came back and ushered us out. He asked my mother if she wanted to ride in the limousine to the graveyard. She said no and asked me to drive us. I was a little surprised, but it hit me that maybe I was the driver now. We got in our station wagon and waited for the casket to be loaded in the hearse.

Ginny wanted to talk. "Why does Aunt Bobby have to be so mean?" she started. It was a question that had been asked over and over in our family for as long as I could remember.

"Not now Ginny," Nana said in a kind voice, trying to stop her.

"She's terrible," Ginny said, almost crying again.

"Well, that has nothing to do with you or us. Your aunt is just that way. You shouldn't let it bother you," Nana tried to explain.

"But she's the only aunt we've got," Ginny said. "She could be nicer."

"She's not going to be," Momma said sternly. "Your Nana is right. It's not you. It's her. It's nothing that any of us did. Can we leave it at that?"

The service at the graveyard was mercifully short. The preacher led us in the Lord's Prayer, and the flag that had been draped over daddy's casket for the ride to the cemetery was folded and handed to my mother. The pallbearers put flowers on the casket and stepped away. My mother got up, and Nana, Ginny, and I followed her away from the gravesite. I heard some commotion behind us, and I turned around to see Aunt Bobby down on her knees, leaning over the casket, sobbing. I know my mother heard it too, but she never turned around.

Chapter 7

I'm having a hard time believing what happened is real. I expect to see the headlights from his truck shining through my bedroom window late at night, to hear the backdoor open, and to hear his slurred voice as he begins to go at my mother with the things he says night after night. Then to hear his heavy footsteps coming near my bedroom door, and finally hearing him fumble around and fall into bed. It's hard to believe that is over. It is hard to sleep. I'm forgetting not to worry about timing my morning routine so I don't run into him before leaving the house. I'm still thinking about what he might do to me and how I might react. I'm forgetting that I won't have to pretend his words don't hurt, and most of all I'm forgetting not to be scared.

...

Ginny and I stayed home from school for the rest of the week. We didn't need to, but Momma and Nana said we should. Ginny was in the sixth grade, and I knew it didn't matter much if she missed a few days at the end of the school year. I had Algebra to worry about and final exams coming up in just over a week. I was also restless. I wanted to get on with something, hopefully something good that could take my thoughts away from the last few days.

Momma opened the store back up just one day after the funeral. She said she couldn't wait any longer. We needed the money. She waited a while to tell us how badly we needed the money. Turns out that Daddy didn't have any life insurance, and he had left some unpaid bills around town too. I spent a couple of long days after the funeral in the store helping her and just being around if she had something to say about all of it. I expected her to talk about Daddy, about the two of them, about how things had gotten so bad between them, about the wreck—anything, but she didn't.

She did talk to me about the radio job. I half expected her to try and talk me into not going up there after all and staying around to help her more at the store, but she didn't. Instead, she seemed more interested in me working there.

"When are you going back up to the radio station?" she wanted to know.

"I've been thinking about it. You still want me to go?" I asked her.

"Why wouldn't I?"

"I don't know, I just thought…" She cut me off.

"I wanted you to do this before, and I want you to do it now. That hasn't changed," she said. "You need to try new things, Neil. We all need to try new things. You don't want to get stuck here."

She surprised me. I don't think I had ever heard her say she was stuck, but of course she was. It should have been obvious that things hadn't turned out the way she expected, or the way she had wanted them to turn out. My grandfather gave her this little grocery store to help our family out where my father wouldn't. I knew it was hard for her, and I figured that she could use my help more than ever now, but it's not what she wanted for me.

"You're sure?" I asked.

"Yes, I am sure. Go and see if you can make this happen. I believe it will be good for you," she said.

"I'll go back up there Saturday then."

I went home and got my little radio from my bedroom

and brought it back to the store to listen while I worked. I put the earplug in and tried to follow what I heard. Billy Brown was on WHJ playing music and talking about what was going on around town. At the top of the hour, he read some local news and gave a long weather forecast, then it was back to "West Tennessee's Best Music on the Big 13-WHJ!" as he seemed to like to say. I had seen enough when I was in the control room to imagine what he was doing, so I could picture myself doing it too. Billy sounded less natural to me than Chris. He was much older, and he had been doing radio for a long time. He said many of the same things over and over. I didn't want to sound like Billy. I knew that much already, but I had no clue how I wanted to sound, or even what kind of sound was possible for me to bring to the radio. The more I listened and thought about it, the more I began to understand how important my sound would be.

I hadn't spoken to anyone at the radio station since the funeral when I showed up there on Saturday morning. I flipped the switch to let Chris know I was at the door, and he came around to let me in. He looked surprised to see me.

"Oh, I didn't know you were... I didn't expect to see you today," he said to me. My father had died, and Chris was the first of many people I would run into for the first time since his death who wouldn't know what to say.

"Come on in," he said. "I made coffee if you want some."

"No thanks, I don't drink coffee," I answered. Chris was only eighteen-years-old, and it surprised me a little that he drank coffee, but he was also smoking a cigarette. It was as if those two things came with the job.

Chris rolled the chair out of production studio and

into the control room for me. He was trying real hard to be nice, and I appreciated it, but I also wanted him to stop. He looked at me like he was searching for a clue as to what he should do next.

"So, you're doing okay?" he finally asked me.

"I'm okay," I answered, trying to sound convincing. "I really am."

He looked at me closely again for a few seconds.

"Okay then, that's good," he said and turned around to get ready to go on the air.

I sat and watched Chris as he played song after song, mostly from tapes on the cart machine. He did play some older songs on the turntable from a stack of 45s that were stored in dark green, heavy paper covers.

"You want to learn to cue a record?" he asked me, while reaching for one of the 45s.

"Sure."

"First, you want to make sure you've got the pot turned down on the board," he said. That was the first time I had heard the word pot used at the radio station. I kind of shook my head when he said it, so he put his hand on one of the knobs on the board and repeated the word.

"Pot, we call these pots," he explained. "Not sure why, I guess they're kind of shaped like a pot. So, you turn down the pot until it clicks into the cue position. Here, feel it," he said and I tried it. "When you feel that click that means you'll be able to hear what you're playing through that pot without it going on the air. That's important."

He put a 45 on the red felt-covered turntable and flipped a small metal switch just to the left of the board forward, causing the turntable to spin, and then he carefully lowered the needle onto the smooth spot at the edge of the record. "Listen," he told me. The needles moved onto the grooves of the record, and I could hear the music begin to play from someplace other than the big speakers hanging on the walls.

"You hear that?" he asked, and I nodded. "That's coming from a little speaker in the board, a cue speaker. What you're hearing is not on the radio. We can hear it; they can't," he said, referring to the listeners. He picked up the needle again, and held it above the edge of the record. "When I hear that first sound I'm going to back the record up almost half a spin," he explained, and dropped the needle back down on the blank edge with his right hand. He held his left hand over the opposite edge of the record and waited for the music to start. "There it is," he said at the first sound and gently put his left hand down on the edge of the record. He pulled it back around past the start of the music. "That's where it starts right?" he said to me. "Now, I'm going back nearly half a turn from there." He turned the record back and flipped off the switch that had started the turntable. "It's cued," he said. "When I hit this switch, the music will start in about half a second. I can time it that way in my head. If you don't pull it back far enough it will drag. If you pull it back too far, it'll take too long to start. About half a second, that's what you want," he said, and turned around to announce the record for his listeners.

"I don't know if it's the sunshine or the moonshine, but things are looking pretty bright around here! That's America on WHJ. I'm Chris Sanders on a Saturday morning; it's eighty-four degrees at ten-forty-two. Hey, no need to stand up straight this morning, here's Bill Withers and you can lean on him!" Chris snapped the microphone switch off and Bill Withers started singing "Lean on Me" on the radio. Chris was only two years older than me, but it was a long way between where I was sitting and what I was watching him do in front of me.

Chris went on to explain how the cue thing worked on all the pots, how you could listen to cart tapes, or reel-to-reel tapes, or even another studio or outside line off air. He went over the things that Woody had said about the tape cartridges, carts they called them. The carts varied in length—anywhere from twenty seconds to five minutes. You could play what was on the carts and the tape inside would keep running around in a circle and then stop automatically where the recording started. All the newer songs and commercials were recorded on carts. There were at least a hundred of them filed in racks to the right of the board.

There was a lot to learn, but maybe not too much. Woody had said it and Chris too, learning to work the buttons and switches and so forth shouldn't be too hard. Learning to sound good on the radio would be the challenge. What if I didn't really have anything to say? That could end this job before it started.

I left the station around noon and walked across the courthouse lawn towards the drugstore. I wanted to see if Angie, Ben, and Coy were there, but I wasn't sure that I wanted to talk to them yet. I imagined there would be some awkward moments to get past with the three of them. I hated the idea of putting them and me in that situation, but I knew too that we had to do it at some point. I stopped and sat on a bench beside the courthouse and stared at the drugstore. I couldn't see through the glass, and the three of them always parked their cars around back, so I couldn't tell who was there working.

So I just sat and thought. I thought about what I had just watched at the radio station. I thought about what my mother had said about me working there, and of course I thought about my father. I had seen his body at the funeral home, and yet it was still impossible to believe he was dead and gone. I wondered how long it would take to accept that he was really gone. I couldn't help but imagine again that this all might be a dream, and that I might wake up any moment and see him staring down at me.

I was staring up in the trees, watching the wind blow, and thinking about all of that so I didn't notice Angie walking toward me across the courthouse square.

"I saw you sitting there from inside the store," she called out. "Why don't you come in?"

"I was just thinking," I answered.

"Oh you were?" she said and sat down on the bench beside me. "Were you thinking about me?" she asked smiling.

I should have said yes, that I thought about her a lot, but I didn't. Instead I said, "I was wondering if you were working."

"Well, I am. What are you doing up here? You been to the radio station?"

"Yeah, I was watching Chris. He's really good," I told her.

"Is he? I hadn't really noticed that much. I hardly ever listen to WHJ."

I wondered if that were true, or if she was just trying to make me feel less insecure about what I was trying to do.

"I don't know if I can do what he does," I said, kind of surprising myself at how honest I was being.

"How long has he been working up there?" she asked

me.

"A couple of years."

"You don't think you will be as good as he is in a couple of years?"

"I don't know. I really don't know," I answered.

"Well, I think you will be, and besides, you won't know until you've tried," she said. That last part she said was true. I wouldn't know until I really tried. That first part though, I knew she was just being nice.

"I've got to get back to work. Come on over and I'll fix you something—my treat."

"I don't think so. Thanks anyway."

She looked closely at me. "Call me if you want to talk, okay?"

"Okay, I will."

I left the square after Angie went back to work and walked down to our store. Momma was behind the counter, and Nana was sitting in her usual place—the big chair beside the store's front window. I looked at the two of them and thought if you didn't know better, you might think nothing had changed.

"You ready to be on the radio?" Nana said, and smiled.

"Oh no ma'am," I answered her. "That won't be for a while, maybe a long time."

"I bet you're closer than you think. You're a smart boy Neil," she added. Momma looked at me without reacting. I could tell she didn't want me to sound negative about the radio job. "I'll tell you what," Nana said. "When you start working at that radio station, you can use my car. I don't drive it anyway. You'll need it for your job. You can't be walking to work all the time."

My mother interrupted her.

"Are you sure you want to do that Momma?"

"When is the last time I drove the car?" Nana asked.

"I know, but you might still need it."

"I've been thinking about it, and I'm pretty much done with it," she said. "He'll get a lot more use out of it now. One of you can give me a ride if I really need one. That's what you do now anyway."

Nana owned a ten-year-old Ford Galaxie sedan. She and my grandfather bought the car new when I was just five-years-old. It was the only car I ever remembered him driving. The car was big and white, with lots of chrome, and a red imitation-leather interior. They stopped making cars that looked like that one a couple of years later. Their car was in good shape. My grandfather had taken very good care of it, but it looked old, very old, and out of style.

I immediately thought about how old the car looked when she surprised me by saying I could use it. My mother might have figured that out when I didn't react.

"You are going to need a car for work," Momma said, "and you could help by getting your sister to school in the morning and running errands for me and your grandmother. Nana is being very generous Neil."

It didn't take me long to think through things a little bit while my mother was talking. I realized in the next moment that this would probably be the only chance I would have to get a car for a while, job or no job, and that I better start sounding grateful. I mean a car was a car. A lot of kids my age were never going to get their own car of any kind.

"Yes ma'am, I know she is. That would be great

Nana," I told my grandmother. "I'll have my license next month. That's great," I repeated.

"Finish school, get your license, and get your job, and you'll have a car to drive this summer," she told me.

"I will," I answered.

...

I stopped by my locker at school first thing Monday morning and found a note taped to the front of it saying I should report to the guidance office before going to class. I was sure this had to do with my father's death, but I hoped the guidance counselor, Mrs. Wortham, wouldn't try to make me feel better. I wasn't sure how I felt, but I didn't want to try to feel better, and I didn't think I had much to say about it at the moment.

Turns out she didn't try to make me talk about it. She was very kind though, and I appreciated her trying to help. Mostly I appreciated what she had to tell me about final exams. After saying how sorry she was about my father, she explained the school's policy about something like this happening so late in the school year.

"Neil, I don't want you to worry about school. You've got a lot to think about and to work through. I've talked to all your teachers, and they agree. You can do as much as you want to this week, but we're not going to make you take final exams. I know you are a little behind this semester in Algebra, but if you agree, we're going to give a final grade of C and leave it at that for the year."

If I agree! I couldn't get it out of my mouth fast enough.

"Yes ma'am, I appreciate that," I answered.

She looked closely at me to see if I wanted to say anything else, but I didn't.

"If there is anything I can do for you, or anything anyone else here at the school can do for you, please come and tell me, Neil. You can call me at home if you need to. We're here to help you," she said, and I believed her. I just couldn't think of anything else. I didn't have to worry about school anymore this year. That's all I could think of, and I was trying not to smile at the thought. I was trying not to jump up and hug her. Maybe I should have.

Instead, I thanked her and left her office. First period had already started and the halls were empty. Thinking about what she just said, I believe I could have turned and walked out of school at that moment and no one would have said a thing. I was tempted to leave. They would have thought I was too upset to face school, and it would have been okay. I could have stayed away for the rest of the school year, but it would have been a big lie.

I walked to the door of my first period class and looked inside. It was Mrs. Owens' English class. We were reading Shakespeare's Julius Caesar before my father's death and they were still on it. Books were open and all the kids were looking down. I knew they would look up when I pushed the door open, and I tried to think of the best way to react when they saw me. I would try to not look too sad, but of course I would try not to smile either. I stood there trying to work it out in my head when Mrs. Neal noticed me and waved for me to come inside.

"Good morning Neil, welcome back," she said to me as I walked across in the front of the class and to my desk in the back of the room. Angie, Coy, and Ben were there. Coy and Ben looked at me without expression; Angie smiled, and I tried to smile back at her. I looked around the room and saw that no one else was looking at me.

The class started back into Julius Caesar. Some of the kids read passages, and Mrs. Neal asked for comments. I couldn't follow much of anything that was being said. I was distracted by the idea that my school year was already pretty much over. I didn't have to keep up with any of this, and there would be no more tests. It didn't seem quite right, but I was more than okay with it.

I sat and replayed the last few days in my mind. I thought about the radio station and about the summer to come. I thought about Angie and tried not to stare over at her while I did. I wondered if my father's death might help me with Angie, that she might think about me more because of it, and maybe that could even help me get a date with her. I should have been ashamed of those thoughts, but I wasn't. So I wasn't paying attention late in the period when Mrs. Neal told everyone to put away Julius Caesar for the day. I didn't hear if she said why, but she started talking about forgiveness.

"Poets and writers of all kinds have wrestled with the idea of forgiving," she said. "Here's something Shakespeare said. *Pray you know, forget and forgive.* Not easy though, forget and forgive. He also wrote, *It is in the pardoning that we are pardoned,* very strong and a lot to think about," she added. "And how about Alexander Pope writing two hundred years later, *To err is human, to forgive is divine.* Forgiveness. Writers, philosophers, you and I, we all struggle with it. Perhaps we know instinctively that forgiveness is good. Good for the soul maybe, but we have a hard time with it. Some things are easier to forgive than others."

"Here's a woman, Emily Bronte writing, *Forgiveness is the mightiest sword. Forgiveness of those you fear is the highest reward.* Back to Shakespeare, here he talks about letting go of hate and moving on:

Love me or hate me, both are in my favor.
If you love me, I'll always be in your heart.
If you hate me, I'll always be in your mind.

"He's saying, I think, if you hold on to hate, you will poison your own mind. Something to think about. And of course Jesus says, *Father forgive them for they know not what they do.*

Well, there it was. Mrs. Neal knew more about me than I ever would have guessed. And she was right. It would help if I could forgive my father—forgive him for threatening and terrorizing my mother, my sister, and me, for never being around to help any of us with anything, and for driving off a bridge drunk and killing himself, making it impossible for him to ever do better by us.

There were only a few seconds left in the period and several of the kids around me were staring at the clock, waiting for the bell. I stopped watching the clock and looked at Mrs. Owens instead. Her eyes were already fixed on me. She smiled and nodded her head just a little as if to say, "it will be alright." I'm not sure, but I think I might have shaken my head no, just slightly, in response.

The bell rang, and Ben, Coy, and Angie crowded around me as we left the room and walked towards our second period class.

"What was that all about?" Coy asked. "Forgiveness is the mightiest sword? What's she talking about? The mightiest sword is the mightiest sword."

Ben laughed. "You've got it all figured out, as usual," he said to Coy.

"I'm just saying I guess you should try to forgive people, but so what. There are a bunch of people I don't like for good reason, and I don't plan on forgiving any of them."

"You know she's right," Angie said, exasperated. "Haven't you ever been to church?" she asked Coy.

"I know, I know. That's what they say in church, but they say a lot of things in church that people don't do."

"At least you can try," she said. "What do you think Neil?" she asked me.

"I don't know, and I don't know why she was talking about it today," I said sharply. I was lying, but I didn't want to say anything else about it. The three of them picked up on that and let it go.

"You need a ride home after school?" Angie asked me. I wasn't expecting her to say that, and I was a little stuck for an answer. She had never offered before, and for a second I wondered what had changed, but of course what had changed was my father's death.

"Sure, that would be great," I finally answered.

"I'll meet you at my car then," she told me.

I nodded and looked over at Ben and Coy. Ben had raised his eyebrows at me, and Coy whispered "okay." Angie ignored both of them.

The rest of the school day went pretty well. A few kids did work up the courage to tell me they were sorry about what had happened. I know it was hard for them. I told them thanks and tried to let it go at that. A couple of teachers quietly told me not to worry about finals and offered to help me any way they could. I tried to tell them all that I was okay, and I felt like I was okay. I didn't feel particularly sad. It all felt strange. Things had changed a lot, but I wasn't sure about all the ways they had changed, or why.

I had lunch with Coy and Ben. The lunchroom was segregated, by choice. Black kids sat on one side, and the white kids sat on the other. There was almost no mingling. Ben liked to get a table on the border of the black and white divide. Some of his black friends would stop by to say hello, and occasionally one would even join us at his table.

Some of the boys who usually ate lunch with us didn't come by. I think they wanted to give the three us a chance to talk since we were best friends, and they might have felt even more uncomfortable about things. So the three of us ate together, and right away I felt like Ben and Coy were just sitting and watching me, maybe looking for a clue about what to say. It was getting a little awkward, which almost never happened between the three of us. I decided to try and get it out in the open.

"Look guys, I'm okay," I started. "I don't want this to get weird. What happened, happened, and I don't know what to say about it right now."

Ben started to try and talk. "Well, I just…you know…"

"Yeah, I know," I said. "If there's something I'll tell you, but I just don't know right now. I think it would be better if we just talked about things we usually talk about." Of course, when I said that none of us could come up with anything to say.

Ben finally said, "Blue Chevy" and smiled. Coy chimed in, "Yeah, the Blue Chevy, my man Neil." They were talking about Angie's car, and I had to laugh. That let them laugh too, and we all felt a little more at ease.

The final bell was slow to come. It was always slow to come, but last period seemed to drag on longer than usual. I was going to meet Angie after seventh period, and I could hardly sit still as the minutes on the clock crawled by. I imagined what I would say to her, and I wondered too if she had something in particular she wanted to say to me. We hadn't talked about my father since that night at the funeral home.

The great relief that was seventh period bell finally came. It was one of those moments in every school day when you could sense how everyone felt. That feeling was relief that another school day was done, and during this particular week, we were sensing how much closer we were to the end of the school year. There was a lot more smiling in the hallways.

I tried not to look like I was rushing too much as I headed down the hall towards the school's back parking lot. If I had let my true feelings show, I would have run to the door and out to where Angie parked her car. I did beat her to the car and then tried to figure how I would pose myself for when she saw me standing there. I leaned up against the front of the car and pulled my foot back on the bumper. I was trying to look cool, and I felt stupid trying.

Then I saw her on the sidewalk just outside the back door of the school. She was walking with a couple of her friends. I felt myself getting tense as she got closer to the car. She stopped and said a couple of things to her friends before turning to me.

"You ready?" she asked me.

"Sure."

"I've got a little time before work, you want to stop by the drive-in for a minute?" she asked.

"Well sure, I've got some time too," I said and quickly

began to assess my money situation. I had a little change in my pocket, but not much, probably not enough to buy myself anything, much less for the two of us. I should have just said I didn't have much money, but I didn't. I sat there and fretted about it.

We got in the car, and I tried not stare at her, but it was hard not to. She was so pretty—long brown hair and green eyes with brown around the center. She was about as tall as me, with long legs that stretched out from under the green skirt she was wearing. When she sat down to drive, the skirt came up several inches above her knees.

Don't stare, I kept telling myself. We pulled into Sam's, and Angie started to get out of the car.

"I'm gonna get a coke. You want one?" she asked.

"Yeah, sure. Let me see how much..." I said and started to dig in my pocket.

"My treat," she said and smiled. I kept digging like I was expecting to find enough money to pay.

"You sure?"

"Yes, I am sure," she said and walked towards the window to order.

Angie came back with a couple of cokes, and we sat and watched kids circle Sam's in their cars on the way out of school. I tried to make eye contact with all of them, and I even waved at a couple of kids from our class. That was not something I would normally do, but I wanted to be seen sitting with her.

"I was thinking about English class," she said to me after of couple of minutes sitting quietly in the car. "Why do you think Mrs. Neal decided to talk about forgiveness all of a sudden?"

"I don't know," I said, not willing to tell her what I thought and what I knew.

"Really?" she asked and looked over at me closely. "I wondered if it had something to do with you coming back to school, but that didn't make sense. Or was there someone else in the class that she knew needed to forgive somebody or be forgiven."

"I don't know," I repeated and shrugged my shoulders slightly. "I guess we all need to be forgiven for something. How about you?"

"What do I need to be forgiven for?" she asked rhetorically. "Probably a lot of things. I could be nicer to my brother," she said and kind of giggled. "I kind of like to torture him, especially when he gets on my nerves." Angie had a little brother about the same age as Ginny.

"I don't think that counts. You don't seriously torture your brother, do you?"

"Maybe not."

"What then?" I asked. "What would you need to be forgiven for? You ever stolen anything?"

"Not really, you?"

"Well, I took a baseball that somebody left at the baseball field one day. I knew it wasn't mine, but I took it home anyway," I told her.

"Is that stealing?" Angie asked.

"It's kind of like stealing, I think," I answered.

"It still doesn't sound like something you have to be forgiven for," Angie said. "I think it has to be something bad you do to somebody or something bad they do to you. You asked to be forgiven or you forgive them, right?'

"I guess so. There is stuff that happens that you don't

forget and that you stay mad at somebody about. That happens to everybody," I said.

"Who are you mad at?" Angie asked, sounding like she knew I had an answer.

"I don't know."

"No, tell me. Who do you need to forgive?" she said.

I couldn't tell her that what our teacher had said let me know that some of the grownups in town—maybe a lot of them—knew about my father. And I couldn't tell her that Mrs. Neal knew that I would need to forgive my father someday, that I would be angry and sad until I could do that. I couldn't say that to her, because I would wind up having to explain it all, and it would sound awful. I didn't know much of anything about Angie's family, but I knew it wasn't like mine, and that she would likely have a hard time understanding. I didn't answer, so we sat there quietly for a bit longer.

"You want to talk about your father, about what happened? I'm just saying that if you want to, it's okay. I can listen," she said and smiled.

"I don't think so Angie. I don't really know what to say about it yet. Maybe some other time. I don't know."

"Okay," she said sweetly. "In the meantime I'll have to figure out whether or not I want to be seen with a boy who would steal a baseball," she said, and laughed. I laughed too. She was funny and smart, and the best thing about the moment was that she had just said something about being seen with me, and I really liked the way that sounded. I imagined us being seen together in other places at other times, and I kept smiling.

"I better get to work," she said, and we pulled away from Sam's. "You're going to work?" she asked. I nodded, and we headed to the store for her to drop me off. "You're getting your license soon?" she asked.

"June 25th," I said, and wondered if I should, or how I should tell her, about Nana's car.

"My grandmother is going to let me use her car when I get my license," I sort of blurted out. "I'll probably use it until I can get my own car, a better car."

"What kind of car is it?" Angie asked.

"It's an old Ford," I said, and I must have sounded apologetic.

"Well, I drive an old Chevy," she said, "nothing wrong with that."

"I'm not saying it is," I said, flustered. I hadn't thought it through, and now she read something into what I said that I didn't intend. I believed that girls cared less about what kind of cars they drove anyway. Turns out she was kidding with me.

"I'll race your old Ford with my old Chevy anytime. You boys think too much about your cars," she said.

"Yeah, maybe. It's a big old car that my grandfather used to drive," I explained. "My grandmother thought I could use it if I get the job at the radio station."

"When you get the job Neil," she corrected me. "When you get the job."

"We'll see. You sound a lot more sure about it than I feel about it," I said.

"No reason I shouldn't sound like that, and there's no reason you shouldn't either," she said matter-of-factly.

Angie was pulling for me, and I liked it, a lot. I should have told her how much I appreciated it, but I didn't. We stopped in front of the store, and I did tell her thanks for the ride. She smiled and told me again that she would be happy to give me a ride anytime, but then she thought more about it.

"I guess you won't be needing rides when you get that big Ford." It made me wonder if I even wanted the thing, if I could ride around with her all the time. But of course I wanted it. Who wouldn't want to own his own car, a grandmother hand-me-down or not?

Nana was inside the store with Momma. Momma asked me about school, and I told her what the guidance counselor told me about not having to take final exams. She was surprised.

"I didn't think about that," she said. "Maybe you want to take some of your finals to pull your grades up." I wanted to ask if she was crazy. Instead, I told her I was okay with my final grades the way they were, and she dropped it. She looked at me for a few moments, and I sensed there was something else she wanted to say.

"Neil, Nana and I have been talking. I think we're going to have to move in with her." She paused and watched me, waiting to see how I would respond. "We're just not making enough money to keep the house, and I've got some bills your daddy left that I'm going to have to pay."

There it was. I was going to have to move out of my house because of my father. I hadn't sorted all out my feelings about him dying, and now I was getting angry. My mother tried to say something to make it better.

"You can have your own room at Nana's house, and you can use her car too," she said. "It'll be all right. I promise you."

"Son of a bitch," I blurted it out.

"What did you say?" Momma asked. She heard what I said.

"That son of a bitch—sorry son of a bitch," I said

again.

Momma started to cry, and Nana tried to shut me up.

"Neil, that won't help," she said. "Please don't upset your Momma."

"I don't know why we stayed with him anyway." I couldn't stop. "He was awful and people around here knew it," I said, thinking about what Ms. Neal said in class today. "Why would anybody marry him?" I said, trying to sound as hateful as I could. I knew it wasn't my mother's fault, but I didn't have anybody else to blame.

"You don't know everything. You might think you do, but you don't," my mother said through her tears.

"I know how he treated you. You know how he treated me. What else do I need to know about a sorry bastard," I told her.

She screamed. "Stop it. That's enough. You don't understand, and I don't want to hear anything else out of your mouth right now." She was the only person who knew how tough it had been on me—on us—and she could have let me say what I needed to say.

I left the store without saying anything else and started walking towards the square. I didn't know what to say or what to do. I had been mad and now my feelings were hurt. I didn't expect my mother to talk to me that way, but I guess I was guilty of calling her husband, a man she had been with nearly twenty years, a son-of-a-bitch and a bastard. But he was my father, and I felt like it was okay for me to say what I felt, especially now since I had just been told I was going to have to leave the house I had lived in all my life.

I walked quickly toward the square, hoping Ben and Coy were working. Seeing them would help. Angie might be there too. Mostly I wanted to walk off some of the anger I felt. I was thinking about him, and about what I had just said to my mother when she pulled up alongside me in her station wagon. She reached across and rolled down the window next to where I was walking. She was smiling.

"Neil, please get in," she said, and I did. We didn't talk while she drove across town and down the main highway. I didn't have to ask. I knew where she was going.

"Ice cream cone?" she asked as she pulled into the Dairy Queen. I smiled and nodded. Momma got the ice cream, and we sat in the car, eating quietly for several minutes. It was our way. We never really apologized to one another. It wasn't necessary. This is how we made up.

"When are you going back up to the radio station?" she asked, breaking the silence.

"I was just thinking about that," I said. "I don't have exams, so I could go up there tomorrow after school if that's alright with you."

"I think that's a great idea," she said, and just like that we put what happened earlier behind us. "Let's get something for Ginny, and go home."

Momma got an ice cream bar for my little sister and we started for the house. I would stay up late with my little radio tonight and listen, and then repeat some of the things I heard them say. The best part was I could do that without worrying about headlights from a truck pulling up in our driveway, about shouting from down the hall, and about footsteps outside the door of my bedroom.

Chapter 8

Angie gave me a ride up to the square after school. Ben and Coy had teased me about it after last period when I told them I had a ride, but of course they were jealous. They didn't say it, but I'm sure they were also a little jealous about me not having to take finals. Angie was wearing a dress again, and I tried not to look down at her legs too much as we rode towards the square. She turned her radio on to WHJ. I'm sure she did it because of me, because most kids my age didn't listen to the station. Chris was on the radio, and he was playing a song called "The Candy Man" and it was terrible. Angie made a face, and I couldn't blame her. Chris came on after the record ended and took a little shot at it, "WHJ with a little sweetness from Sammy Davis Jr. Maybe a little too sweet for my taste, but that's just me."

"I hope all the music isn't like that," Angie said.

"It's really not. Some of it is pretty good," I answered.

"Yeah, I'm sure it is," she said, realizing she might be sounding too negative. "How long before Chris leaves?"

"I need to ask. He's going off to school at the end of the summer, so I guess he'll work until then. Should give me time to get ready."

"Sure it will," she said with a confidence I wasn't feeling yet.

Angie dropped me off in front of the station and told me, "Good luck, have fun." I told her thanks and headed up the steps towards the studios. I would need the luck, and I didn't think about this as fun, at least not yet. Mrs. Burns was sitting at her desk as usual when I went inside. She was smoking, and a blue cloud hung over her desk. I braced myself for what she might say, but I was surprised. She actually smiled at me.

"Well, hello Neil, good to see you. Glad you made it back up here." I was so surprised by what she said that I was stuck for a response.

"Yes ma'am" I answered quietly.

"Woody's not here. Does Chris know you're coming?" she asked very warmly.

"No ma'am."

"You want me to tell him, or you can just go on back. I'm sure he'll be glad to see you."

"I'll just go on back," I said. "Thanks," and I tried to smile at her a little. I knew why she was treating me that way, and I did appreciate it. I also wanted things to get back to normal with the people around me.

I walked down the hall and looked inside the glass door to the control room. Chris was shuffling through some carts, so I tapped on the glass to get his attention, and he waved me in. I got the chair from the next room and sat it down behind him to watch. I thought about the song Angie and I heard on the way over and decided to poke a little fun.

"I came to see the Candy Man," I said to Chris, who turned around to look at me. I laughed and he smiled.

"Man, that record sucks," he said.

"I could tell you didn't like it. You took a little shot at it."

"Yeah, you have to be careful with that. Woody doesn't like us making fun of the music," he warned me.

"I'll remember," I said.

"You can say some things, but not everything you think. That's for sure. It's the same way with people around town. There are some things you might think about people—things you think would be funny to say, but you just can't say them if you want to work here," he explained.

"Like what?" I asked.

"Well, you can't make fun of anybody who buys spots on the station. And you can't make fun of anybody in government—like the mayor or the police. Don't ever say anything bad about them. You can't say anything bad about the sports teams, or clubs, or anything else going on in town. And when you start doing local news, be real careful with that. Don't read bad stories about the people in town, ever."

"So what can you say? What do you say?" I asked him.

"Here's the thing: You want to sound like you love Harper's Junction and that you're happy to be here. That's what Woody wants, and that's what the guys who own the radio station want," Chris said and turned around to announce his next record.

"That's Robert John and 'The Lion Sleeps Tonight,' just the way I like it. How about we let him sleep this afternoon too, and nobody gets hurt. It's eighty-five degrees in the sunshine of Harper's Junction, feels like one of those Sweet Seasons Carole King loves to sing about so much on WHJ!"

Chris flipped off the microphone switch, dropped his headphones down around his neck, and turned around.

"That's the kind of crap you can say," he said and frowned.

"You said 'the guys who own the station.' Who are the guys who own the station? Woody doesn't own it?" I asked.

"Oh no, Woody works for the guys who do, a bunch of men, the big shots around here own the station."

"Like who?"

"I don't know them all. The mayor and the judge own a piece, and that guy Turner who owns a bunch of stores. I think there are others. So anyway, the thing is you have to keep that in mind when you talk on the radio. They want to hear good things about Harper's Junction, and they don't want to hear bad things about themselves."

"Didn't know that," I said.

"I didn't know it either when I started, but it didn't take long to figure it out. Remember Andy Garrett?"

"Kinda," I answered.

"He was a senior when I was a sophomore, pretty good on the radio. He got into it with Woody and his bosses over some little thing he said about the police."

"What was that?"

"Nothing really, the police caught a guy who had been breaking into houses. They had to chase him, and Andy said something about the police might need to cut back on the donuts if they were going to have to chase bad guys on foot. One of them heard it and didn't like it because he's fat. He called Woody, and Woody told Andy to apologize. Andy wouldn't do it so the police chief told one of the guys who owns the station, I don't know which one, and he made Woody fire Andy. That's how they shut people up."

I didn't want to worry about all that just now. I just needed to learn to do what Chris was doing. I could worry about stuff like that later, if I had to. I sat and watched as Chris worked his way through his shift. He made it look easy. He was busy, but he never seemed to get in a rush, and he was always ready with the next thing to play, or when it was time to talk. I said something to him about being ready.

"That's it," he said. "You have to be loaded and ready. Don't get caught at the last second with nothing ready to play or nothing to say. It'll sound like shit when you do that, and it's the kind of stuff that will give you nightmares."

"Nightmares? Really?" I asked.

"Yeah, nightmares about being on the radio and having nothing—nothing to play, nothing to say. It's the worst thing ever," Chris said. "Maybe you'll have bad dreams about it anyway, but the less you get caught not ready, the better it will be. Get your carts ready, get your record cued up, get your copy in front of you, and then you'll have time to think of all the clever shit you want to say."

There it was. It sounded pretty simple, but I knew it wouldn't be easy, especially at first. I was anxious to get my hands on the equipment and figure some things out for myself. "When do you think I could try some of this?" I asked Chris.

"Whenever you think you're ready. I'm okay with it. You probably want to run the board first before you try to do the whole thing," Chris explained.

"How would I do that?" I asked.

"We can work something out. You run the board and I'll do the talking, something like that," he said. "I'll stand over in the studio with a microphone and do the talking while you play the music and spots from in here. It's not hard, but we need to go over and over all this a lot before we try it."

"Whatever you think," I said. 'Thanks."

Chris did his show and talked me through everything he was doing for the next couple of hours. I watched and listened as closely as possible. I wanted to get on to the next thing. He made it look simple and easy, like anyone who is good at his job. I knew that wasn't true though. I just hoped I could catch on.

I was careful about staying too long. I didn't want to bother Chris. He had been very generous with his help. He even seemed to enjoy being the teacher. Still, I figured I should go. I thanked him and walked over to the drugstore. They would be closing soon. Angie would probably be gone, but Ben or Coy would be there helping Ben's dad close.

The place was empty of customers when I walked in. I could see Mr. Geist behind the pharmacy counter in the back, so I walked towards him. He saw me and called out.

"Neil, come on back," he said. I walked around the counter and up to the platform where he stood to dispense prescriptions. He was counting pills—scraping them from a big pile with a flat metal tool that looked a little like a putty scrapper. I sat down on a tall stool and waited for him to finish. He counted the white pills out in groups of five until he got the number he was looking for and pushed them into a plastic sleeve. Then he poured them out and counted them all again. Satisfied with his count, he put the pills in a small prescription bottle and stepped over to an old manual typewriter to make a label. He two-finger typed the label out and taped it to the bottle of medicine. All done, he turned and looked at me.

"I'll take this to Mrs. Scott on my way home," he said. "You just missed Ben. He had a delivery, and then he was going home. I'm glad you stopped by. How have you been?"

His question sounded different from the way I had been hearing people ask me that lately. It sounded to me like they were saying it because they were supposed to, but Ben's father had always seemed interested in how I was doing, so it didn't hit me that way.

"I'm okay Mr. Geist," I answered.

He nodded. "And how about your mother and sister?"

"Okay I guess, I think so."

"It must be hard. Neil, I won't pretend to know how you're feeling—how they're feeling, but I do want you to know if I you need my help, you just ask me. Okay?"

I couldn't answer. Tears came rushing to my eyes. Mr. Geist gave me a few moments and then tried to change the subject a little.

"So, tell me about the radio station," he said.

"I was just over there," I said. "Chris is helping me."

"You're learning a lot?" he asked me.

"I guess so. There is a lot. I've never thought about how radio works before now, much less how to make it work."

"Neil, I've known you for several years now, and I am sure you can learn how to do that job and be good at that job," he said with a confidence that surprised me. In that moment, I felt like I could believe what he was saying. I was still holding back the urge to cry, so I only nodded my head to answer.

"Hey, I'm closing up in a few minutes. You need a ride home? I can drop you off," he offered.

"I think I'll walk," I said. "Thank you though."

"Well if you're sure, it is a nice evening for a walk."

I sat on the stool for another minute or two watching, while Mr. Geist cleaned up his counter and got ready to leave. I thought about what he said before, and I was ready to answer.

"I think you're right," I said. "I can do that job. Other kids have learned how to do it. I can too."

He turned and grinned at me. "Well then, that's what you'll do. You're on your way."

. . .

The week went by pretty quickly. I went to the radio

station in the afternoons and watched Chris. Angie gave me rides every day. She and I began to talk about different things, all kinds of things. Angie was smart and she was clever too. She followed the news and was interested in what was happening with the war and with the presidential elections. I wasn't ready when she asked me who I supported for president.

"I don't know. I don't like Nixon, and I don't like Wallace," I answered.

"Well, who do you like?" she asked.

"I don't know the others very much. There's Humphrey, but he's already lost to Nixon once. Who else… who do you support?"

"McGovern, I like McGovern. He seems like a good man, and he wants to end the war right away. Mostly, I don't like Nixon. I don't think you can trust him. Just look at him."

"I guess I know what you mean," I said.

"And can you believe Tennessee voted for George Wallace?" she asked.

She was talking about the primary elections that took place in early May. Tennessee had gone all in for Wallace. It wasn't even close. And yes, I could believe it. All you had to do was listen to the people around town to know he was going to win, and why he was going to win. The people around Harper's Junction, the white people anyway, wanted things to "be like they used to be." Whatever that meant. And most of them thought George Wallace could make that happen for them. Wallace was shot and nearly killed a short time after the Tennessee primary. He was left paralyzed and most people didn't think he could be The President anymore.

"I'm sorry for what happened to him," she said, "but I'm glad he won't be president."

"I guess he could still be president," I said.

"Do you think you would vote for George McGovern?" she asked me.

"I can't vote," I said. "I'm not even sixteen-years-old yet."

"If you could, would you vote for him?" she asked, and it seemed important to her.

"I might. I guess it would depend on who else was running," I said.

"Richard Nixon against George McGovern," she said. "Who would you vote for?"

"What if I just decided not to vote," I said, to tease her a little.

"You can't decide that. You have to vote."

"I have to vote? That doesn't sound very American. Why do I have to vote?"

She smiled, knowing I was messing with her. "You have to vote because I say you have to vote. You don't need another reason."

"I might have to go someplace where people didn't force you to vote," I said.

"And where would that be?" Angie asked.

"France, I bet they wouldn't make you vote in France," I said, trying to sound smart.

"Oh, you wouldn't move to France," she said. "I'm sure of that."

"And why are you so sure?'

"Because you're not even sixteen-years-old yet, that's why," she said and laughed.

She had made a good joke, and I laughed too. We were having fun talking and spending time together. I felt lucky about the way things were working out. She found out about the radio job and that seemed to get her interested in what I was doing. Then my father died, and it felt like she was more concerned about me. I should have felt a little guilty about that, but I didn't. I believed she liked me.

Friday was my last day of school. The other kids would be taking exams the next week. I guess I could have felt a little guilty about that too, but of course I didn't feel guilty at all. It was a big relief, especially to be done with Algebra for the year. I left school on Friday with Angie, and we rode to the square in her car.

"How does it feel?" she asked me on the way. I didn't have to ask what she was talking about. She wanted to know how it felt to be through with our sophomore year.

"I don't know. I mean I'm relieved. I think it's going to be a good summer."

"I think it's going to be a very good summer," she said.

"How do you mean?"

"We're sixteen Neil," she smiled and added, "I'm sixteen, you're nearly sixteen. We'll have cars this summer. We'll be driving. It will be a very good summer," she said. "You do know how to drive, don't you?"

"Of course I know how to drive," I said, trying to sound sure of myself. I had gotten my driving permit in January, and I had driven my mother around town a little bit, but I wasn't one hundred percent sure about passing my driver's test. Ben and Coy had told me about it. They said it was pretty easy, that the written test wouldn't be a problem, and the state trooper who gave the driver's test wasn't that interested in how well kids drove. They told me you just drove out to the highway and back, and that was it. The test was coming up for me in a couple of weeks, and I hadn't gotten the little book you needed to study.

"You think you could take me by the state troopers' office real quick? I need to get one of those books for the test," I asked.

"Good idea," she said and turned toward the road leading out to the place.

"You know you can drive my car to get ready for the test," she said as we rode along.

"I don't think you're suppose to do that," I said, knowing you needed someone at least eighteen-years-old with you to drive on a permit. She knew it too.

"It won't matter. We could do it outside of town. No one will care," she said.

"I'm not sure…"

"We're going to have a great summer, and you need some practice driving. You've got that big Ford waiting," she said and smiled again. I couldn't say no.

"Tomorrow, after work we'll drive down to the river," she said. "And you can practice."

"Well, okay," I answered.

I got the little book and Angie dropped me off in front of the radio station. It felt extra good to be done with the school year and heading up the stairs to work. And I was carrying the thought of riding out to the river with Angie. Maybe this would be a great summer.

Mrs. Burns was nice to me again when I passed her desk, maybe not quite as nice as the last few days, but still different than when I first met her. I imagined that she would be back to her old self with me soon, and I was ready for that.

I stopped in front of Woody's office to say hello, before going back to the control room.

"Hey Neil, Chris told me that he thought you were ready to try and run the board," he said to me.

"I think so," I said, and then realized I should have said something a little more positive than that, but it was okay.

"That's good. Chris and Rusty will be gone soon. We'll need some help," he said, repeating what he had told me before.

"I believe I can be ready," I said, trying to muster as much confidence as possible.

"Good, sounds good," he said, and looked back down at the papers on his desk.

I walked on back to the control room and looked inside. Chris had his headphones on and he was sitting up to the microphone. It looked like he was about to talk, so I waited and watched. The light outside the door came on as Chris hit the microphone switch with his left hand. I could hear him from the radio down the hall in the lobby.

"WHJ, great music and more, all day, every day! Here's Glenn Campbell and that Wichita Lineman who's still on the line, when is that guy coming down?"

He always had something to say. I hadn't even started the job and I was fretting about finding things to say. I knocked on the control room door and stepped inside.

"I talked to Woody about you running the board for me," he said.

"Yeah, he told me," I said.

"How about tomorrow morning," Chris asked. "We'll try to start around ten o'clock."

"That's good," I answered, and imagined making

radio, at least kind of, and Angie and I going down to the river together. Tomorrow could be great, or it could be a disaster.

I watched Chris closely for the next couple of hours. I tried to mimic his actions, while sitting behind him without looking too weird. I even took notes and asked a couple of questions about switches on the board that I had wondered about. I didn't feel like I was prepared to sit in his seat and run the board, but I knew it was time. Chris still hadn't told me when exactly he was leaving his job, but I knew it would be soon enough, and I had a lot to learn.

I walked home from the radio station that evening listening to the final hour of Chris' show on my little pocket radio. I could have gotten a ride with him after he was off the air, but I wanted some time to go over what I would have to do in the morning. Had I learned enough and would I know enough to keep his show going in the morning? I wouldn't bet that I had, but I was glad he was willing to risk it for me.

It was nearly dark when I reached our house, and my mother was already home from the store. I had just reached our yard when the back door opened, and she stepped down the steps carrying a large cardboard box. She didn't see me as I watched her walk quickly with the box out to the little garage behind our house. She put it down and then saw me as she turned to go back inside.

"What are you doing?" I asked her.

"Oh nothing," she said. She sounded flustered.

"What's in the box," I asked.

"Just stuff."

"What do you mean, stuff?"

"Okay, it's some of your Daddy's stuff."

"What are you doing with it?" I asked her.

"I'm just taking it out, you know. I'm not really doing anything with it," she said. "You can go through it if you want to."

"I don't know, maybe. I'll think about it."

We went inside and Momma made supper. We sat down to the table, and I started to tell her and Ginny about what I was going to be doing at the radio station the next day. Ginny had a hard time understanding, and I wasn't sure Momma really understood either.

"You run the station and he does the talking?" she asked.

"I guess you could say it that way," I said.

"I never heard of that, but I don't really know anything about it," Momma said.

"I don't either," I answered, "but I guess I'm learning or will learn. It would be real easy to mess this up tomorrow."

"You're not gonna mess up anything," she said. "I'll listen."

"Maybe you shouldn't listen, not to my first time. Give me a chance to figure it out first," I told her. She looked a little hurt at me saying that.

"You don't want me to listen?" she asked

"It's not that. I just don't want everybody hearing me mess up," I said.

"Fine then, I'll wait until you tell me," she said, and dropped it.

She and Ginny settled in on the couch to watch television after supper. I lay down on my bed and listened to the radio, going over and over the steps of what I would have to do at the radio station in the morning. I had things fairly straight in my head, but I also figured that I would feel different when it was really happening, and the pressure was on.

As I tried to focus, my mind wandered to the boxes my mother had taken out to the garage. I knew most of what would be there—clothes and such—but I imagined other things, the more interesting stuff. I had looked in my father's drawers, especially the top drawer, several times throughout my childhood, but I hadn't looked in a couple of years. I had found a whiskey bottle in a drawer before. He kept some old papers in there too, including a couple of letters from his mother that were written to him when he was in the army, a few old photographs—one of him and his army buddies taken before they were shipped off to the Pacific during World War II—and some Army decorations he had received during his service. He also had a couple of old pocket knives that I believed belonged to his father and grandfather. I was interested in all of that as a young boy, and I was still curious about it now.

I was awake when Ginny and Momma went to bed, and I couldn't stop thinking about the stuff in the garage. I got up and walked quietly down the hallway, stopped in the kitchen to get a flashlight, and slipped out the back door. There were about half-a-dozen boxes of stuff there of his that she had taken from the house. I shined the flashlight down on them and began to dig through the stuff. There were several boxes of clothes, along with a box of personal items from the bathroom. I picked up a bottle of Old Spice after-shave and splashed a little bit on my hand. It was his smell, at least his special-occasion smell, and it hit me pretty hard. I thought about that smell and the times I remembered him smelling that way. There were some good times, family gatherings and holidays when things would hold together for a little while, maybe even a few days. But those times always ended, and usually they ended quickly and painfully. He would disappear and then come back more angry and more drunk. At least that's the way it seemed.

I picked up the last box, the smallest one, and started to dig through it. It was the stuff from his top drawer. There was no liquor bottle. He had stopped hiding those years ago. There were two old photographs, one of him and his Army buddies looking happy and fit just weeks before they would be sent into battle, and another of him as a small boy, standing alongside his sister and their parents on the front porch of their tiny old house, which stood a few miles outside of Harper's Junction.

And there were two letters. I picked up the first one and tried to read it. It was from his mother. She had sent it to him while he was in Army basic training.

> *My Sweet Boy,*
>
> *I miss you so much. We all do. Your daddy is sick to death with worry, and he wants you to be very careful at war. I do too of course and your little sister also. If there is anything you need, please let me know, and we will try to get it to you. We are all okay except for missing you. I know you promised me that you would not take any chances, and that you would take good care of yourself while you are gone, and that you would be okay in the Army. Please, please, keep that promise and we will be okay too.*
>
> *Love,*
>
> *Momma, Daddy, and Sister*

The letter was dated March 10, 1943 and was addressed to Fort Riley, Kansas. The second letter was also addressed to Fort Riley, and as I started to read it, I thought I was reading a letter from my mother to him. It wasn't from her though. It was from another girl.

Sweetheart,

It seems like you have been gone forever, even though it's only been a few weeks. My heart aches for you, and I think of you every moment of every day. Please come home to me as soon as possible. I don't think I can bear even one more day without you. I know this is not your choice for us to be apart, and so I will wait for you as long as it takes.

All my love,

Betty

I had no idea who Betty was, but I knew he stayed in the Army a few years after the war, and my parents married less than a year after he came home. I wondered what had become of her, and why they didn't stay together. I put the letters down and continued to dig through the box. There were several pins and decorations in there that I knew were from the Army. Some were shaped like bars, others more rounded, and there were a couple of small medals attached to short ribbons. I put those aside and looked a little more. There was a small pocketknife lying at the bottom of the box that I recognized. It had been in his drawer for as long as I could remember. I think I had been told that it belonged to my grandfather, and he had left it to daddy. That's the way I remembered it, but I wasn't sure. I slipped the knife in my pocket, put the other things back in the box, and went in the house to go to bed. It took me a long time to go to sleep. It was hard to let go of my anxiousness about

what I was going to be doing tomorrow—the radio station and
driving Angie's car. On top of that I was very curious about the
letter to my father from Betty. I wondered how I could find out
about her without having to ask my mother.

Chapter 9

I dug around longer than usual trying to find the right shirt to wear to the station and for seeing Angie. I tried on most of my shirts and settled for the dark blue one with red dots. It had the tallest collar, and I liked the way it looked. I brushed my hair back and forth, trying to make it look as long and thick as I could. Then I thought about covering my biggest zit with some colored cream that was supposed to help your complexion, but never really did. I decided not to use it because it also made you look like you were wearing makeup, and I didn't want that.

I left the house and crossed the street to the store. My mother had already opened up, and I wanted to get something to eat before I went to the radio station. I went in, got a honey bun and soft drink, and sat down beside her behind the counter.

"I looked through those boxes last night," I told her.

"Yeah, I heard you out there," she said. "You find anything you want to keep?"

"I got that pocket knife. I think it belonged to Granddaddy," I said.

"Yes, he would want you to have it," she said. "I mean your grandfather would want you to. Anything else?"

I was tempted to ask her about the letter and about Betty, but I decided not to. I figured I might be stirring something up if I did. Though the thing was, she probably knew that I saw it. Still, I let it go.

"No, not really."

"I kept back some things for Ginny. If you're through with it, I'm going to tell your aunt she can have whatever she wants from what is left. There's not much."

"Sure," I answered. I did wonder why she was moving his stuff out of the house now and it hit me that she might be getting us ready to leave.

"Are we moving?" I asked her.

"I told you we were," she said.

"I mean soon."

"Pretty soon. I don't have the money to stay in our house."

"I've got to go," I said and headed for the door. I heard her say "sorry Neil" as I stepped outside. I should have turned around and said something to make her feel better, but I didn't.

I turned my little radio on, hooked up the earpiece, and walked towards the square. The music on WHJ was okay. There was Al Green, Neil Diamond, and The Carpenters. I was also starting to notice more and more what they didn't play at WHJ—no Rolling Stones, no Led Zepplin, nothing I would call rock music. Chris was on the air, sounding happy with what he was playing and what he was saying. I knew he didn't feel exactly the way he sounded. I got to the station and flipped the switch beside the door to let Chris know I was outside waiting.

"You ready to try this?" he asked when he let me in.

"I think so. Yeah, I'm ready to try," I said, trying to build some confidence.

"Let's do it then," he said.

We walked back to the control room and Chris started to go over everything again—the microphone switch, the cart machines, the turntables, the reel-to-reel tape machines, the program log, the transmitter log, all of it. He had also written down a list of songs we would play over the next two hours, some on carts and some records.

The clock seemed to speed up as we moved towards ten o'clock and the hour I would start running the board for Chris. He kept repeating everything he was doing and everything I would be doing. My hands were sweating, and I could hear my heartbeat in my ears. If I felt this nervous about just pushing buttons and flipping switches, I couldn't imagine how I was going to react when I started talking on the radio.

Chris put the network newscast on at ten and looked back at me.

"Okay?"

"Yeah, okay," I said.

Chris got up and moved towards the control room door.

"I'm gonna prop the door open," he said. "I can get back in here easier that way if I need to. News, jingle, song," he said and I nodded.

There was no one else in the radio station, so we didn't worry about sounds from the other rooms when the microphone was on. Chris walked around to the other side of the studio and sat down at a stool facing the control room glass. I was slow to sit down in the control room chair after he left. I stood there for a few seconds, trying to get my thoughts together. I looked up at Chris and saw him talking to me. I couldn't hear him yet, but I read his lips. "Let's go!" I nodded and looked down at the music list for the first hour.

I sat down, pulled on the headphones, and reached over to grab the first carted song I would need to start the hour. I could barely make my arm and hand work. It felt like I was going in slow motion and that the cart was moving itself to where I needed it to go. I finally slid it into the player and pulled the lever back to lock it in place. *Good*, I thought, *at least I'm ready to start the hour.* The clock was counting up to four minutes past. I was going to turn down the news at five past ten, start the song, and turn on the microphone for Chris. With twenty seconds to go, I looked over at Chris who was gesturing at the cart rack. It took me a second to figure out what he was trying to tell me. He started yelling and I could hear him just a tiny bit from the open door behind me. "Jingle! Jingle! Jingle!"

I already forgot I was supposed to play a station jingle between the news and the song. Chris was watching me and saw that I had put the song cart in, but hadn't gotten a jingle ready to play. Now with less than thirty seconds to go until the newscast, I was fumbling around for the right cart. I could feel the seconds ticking down, and it was distracting me from getting my hand on the right cart. I thought I heard the newsman on the network finishing as I spotted the cart I needed to load and play. I grabbed it, slammed it onto the machine, and turned to look at Chris. He was looking across at me through the glass with his hands held up over his head and his eyes wide open.

"Go!" he was yelling again. I didn't have to hear him. I knew what he was saying, and in a brief moment I knew why. I realized there was no sound in my headphones. The newscast had ended, and the two of us were sitting there in silence—no news, no jingle, no song, no Chris. I fumbled for the button on the cart machine and hit it. The recording of a group singing "WHJ" came into my headphones, and I tried to get my hands to do what I needed to do next. The singers finished, and I hit the start button on the machine I had loaded my song in. *Okay, jingle, then song, now I need to get Chris on*, except I was too slow. Chris' microphone should have already been on. I glanced up at him just as I flipped the switch to put him on the air, and he was waving his hands above his head again. I could see the frustration in his face as he finally got to introduce the song.

"1330-WHJ. Chris here with some sweet soul from the Staple Singers. This is 'I'll Take You There,' and I hope Mr. Robinson over there will do that for us this morning. Take us there, Neil." He smiled a little after he said it, I think because he was happy he had come up with something clever to say on the spot after my slow start.

Chris looked across at me and tapped his headphones. He wanted me to put his microphone in audition so he could talk to me off-air. I flipped the microphone switch and the studio speaker control knob over to audition.

"Little bumpy," he said. "Not a big deal. People aren't listening that closely. We've got two more songs and then some spots coming up, right?" he asked, and I nodded yes. "That second song is a record. Get that one cued up as soon as you can, so you won't have to worry about it."

I put another song cart in and turned to the stack of records Chris had picked out for me earlier. I pulled the 45 labeled "My Girl-The Temptations" from its green sleeve and placed it down on the felt-covered turntable with my left hand and flipped the switch to get it turning. I picked up the arm to place the needle on the record and realized I was shaking, and that I was going to have a hard time placing the needle down on the right spot to hear the beginning of the record. I tried to ease it down, but I had to start and stop several times to get close to the right spot.

When I finally dropped the needle onto the right spot and let it move across and into the grooves of the record, the opening moments from "My Girl" were blending in with "I'll Take You There." I had forgotten to turn the knob controlling the sound from the turntable all the way down into the cue position, and the music from the turntable was on the air at the same time as the music from the cart machine. *Two big mistakes in less than ten minutes, what a start.* I imagined Woody listening as I snapped the turntable output knob down into the cue position. I didn't look up at Chris to see his reaction to my screw-up. The music from the record was now coming through the tiny cue speaker, but it was too late to pull the record back to the right place without picking up the arm up and setting the needle back to the start.

This was all taking time and my first song was running out. I glanced up at the clock and over at Chris just in time to realize that I needed to pay attention to the board again and not worry about the record until after I started the next song. I put the turntable arm back on its cradle and tried to think about what I should do next. It was all happening very fast. I hit the switch to turn on the microphone for Chris and realized that my hands were sweaty. I wiped my hands on my pants and got Chris on the air just as The Staple Singers faded out. I looked over at the cart machine and fumbled a little before hitting the green start button to get the next song going as Chris did his thing.

I don't know what he said on the air next. I don't really remember anything he said for the next two hours. I was thinking about turning this down and turning this thing up, and flipping this switch on and flipping the next one off. Things started to go a little better. I got the record cued and the carts lined up to play the commercials coming up. I was forced to think very hard, and to concentrate on every move, but I was also getting past the near panic I felt when the hour started.

There were bumps. I didn't hit the jingle quickly enough coming out of the commercials, one of the records I cued up started a little slowly, and a couple of other things didn't work out exactly right. Still, with all that, as the first hour ended and my second hour started, I began to feel like I was kind of getting the job done. Chris talked me through it all, and I couldn't have made it through that first shift without his help. It would have been much easier for him to do it himself and have me try to learn by just watching. I should have told him how much I appreciated it, but I only thanked him when we were done.

We kept things going together until noon. Two hours felt like plenty—like a lot, really. I wanted to get outside and try to breathe normally again. Chris had two more hours to go on the air.

"You want to try this again, or do want to do the whole thing next time?" he asked me as I got ready to leave.

"I'm not sure," I answered. "Let me think about it."

"Whatever you want to do. Just tell me."

I walked over to Sonny's Café on the square to get a hamburger and replay everything that happened at the radio station. Angie was getting off work at two o'clock, and I would meet her then. I stepped into Sonny's and sat down near the front window. There was one man all the way in the back, playing pool and only a couple of people eating. I could hear WHJ on somewhere in the back. A song by Blood, Sweat and Tears was playing.

A waitress who had been there ever since I could remember, a woman everyone called Momma Mina, came and took my order. I had a funny urge to tell her what I had just been doing, but I didn't. She called me "sweetie" and asked, "what can I get you?" I ordered a burger and fries and sat looking out the front window across to the square to the second story window of the radio station.

You couldn't see in the window with the sun reflecting against it, but of course I could picture Chris sitting in there with his headphones on waiting to hit the microphone switch. Just then his voice came on from the radio playing in the café. When I Die or leave this radio station, whichever comes first," he said. "That's Blood, Sweat and Tears which is what I planned to leave behind on 1330 WHJ." He gave the weather forecast and the temperature before starting the next song. Chris was hinting at leaving again, and it sounded like he might not last the whole summer.

I ate my burger and thought about the radio station and the people who listened to it. There it was on in Sonny's place, and my mother listened some too, so did a lot of the parents of kids my age. They all liked to listen to the local news that came on in the early morning with Woody. There wasn't a daily newspaper in Harper's Junction, and a lot of people in town got their daily news—things like funeral notices and reports on fires and car wrecks—from WHJ. And even though not many kids my age listened, the station was important to the town, and that made what I was trying to do seem important too. I knew I should treat it that way.

I sat for a while after I finished eating, sipping on my coke and listening to the talk at the one table near me where two men were having lunch. They were talking about George Wallace and what to do next now that he had been shot and paralyzed. One of them said that he could never be elected president now in the shape he's in. The other one said he couldn't see much other choice with "them other Democrats." Neither one of them mentioned George McGovern by name. They did talk about the president. "I had to hold my nose and vote for Nixon the first time," one said. "I guess I'll have to do it again, or stay home."

I saw someone moving toward the door from the back of the café. It was the man who had been playing pool alone. I hadn't paid attention to him when I came in. It was Barry Owens. Barry had been to Vietnam. He and his best buddy joined the Army after high school. His buddy was killed in Vietnam, and Barry came back home to live after the Army. He had worked at the radio station during high school, and had been working there some since he got back home.

I had never met him. I did see him every now and then driving around in an old 1950s style car with fins and chrome wheels. I believe it was the same car he drove in high school. He had let his hair grow since the Army. It was long, down nearly to his shoulders and he had a beard too. He stuck out in Harper's Junction, and he scared some people, maybe just by the way he looked.

The men at the table said hello to him as he came by. He nodded and said nothing. He saw me next and seemed to look very closely at me. I saw the name on the Army jacket he was wearing. It was Garrett, not Owens. Garrett was the name of his best friend who lost his life in Vietnam.

"Hey kid," he said to me, and seemed to try to smile.

"Uh… hi," I managed to say.

I watched him leave the café and walk out to his old hot rod. I could hear it crank from inside the café. Barry backed the car quickly out onto the street, and peeled out with a loud squealing of the tires. One of the men sitting nearby commented.

"I'm afraid that boy has come a little undone," he said.

"It's a real shame," the other one added.

I paid my bill and walked over to the other drugstore on the square, not the one where Angie worked. I thought about Barry and wondered how undone he might really be, and I thought about what Angie had said about McGovern. She said he wanted to end the war quickly. All I knew about the election was I didn't like Nixon, and I sure didn't like Wallace.

The ladies who worked the front counter didn't mind if you looked at magazines for a while without buying. I picked up a copy of Time magazine and looked for any news about McGovern. There were two stories about the presidential campaign. One said McGovern had won in Oregon and had a chance to be the Democratic nominee for president if he could win in California next week. Another story said he had picked up endorsements from Coretta Scott King and Cesar Chavez. I knew that King was the wife of Martin Luther King Jr., but I knew nothing about Chavez. I wasn't sure if I had even heard his name. The article said he was known for helping farm workers in California get better working conditions and better pay. That sounded like a good thing. Most importantly, I had a couple of things I could tell Angie about McGovern, and I expected her to like that, maybe even be impressed by it.

I hung around the magazine stand until it was time to meet Angie at her car. I smiled at the lady working the front counter who had been watching me. She smiled back, so I felt like I hadn't stayed too long without buying something. I left and walked around behind the buildings on the square where Angie left her car, and waited. It was nearly two o'clock and I expected to see her come out of the drugstore any second. I hadn't planned on seeing Coy pull up in his old truck before she came out.

"What are you sneaking around back here about?" he said with a grin. "You're not waiting on the girl who drives that blue Chevy, are you?" I didn't answer, but it occurred to me to say, "you're just jealous," which he might have been.

"I've been over at the radio station," I said, trying to deflect the Angie talk.

"Oh yeah, how did it go?" Coy asked.

"I don't know. It could have been better. It could have been worse."

"Did you talk on the radio?"

"No, I just ran the board for Chris," I said.

"What does that mean?"

"I played the songs and the commercials and stuff, and he did the talking."

"When are you going to say something? You can't work in radio without saying something, can you?"

"No, not really. Pretty soon, I think. I've just got to make myself do it."

"I guess it would probably be hard the first time," he said. "I've got to get inside. You want to do something tonight?"

"Yeah, I should be home," I answered.

"You should be? Maybe I should check with Angie," he said, grinning again.

"Maybe you should," I said, trying to sound more confident about things with Angie than I should have.

"Maybe you should what?" asked a voice from behind us. I hadn't noticed that Angie had walked up near enough to hear us and now wanted to know what I was talking about.

"Nothing, nothing really," I said, trying not to turn red with embarrassment.

"Mr. Geist is looking for you," she said to Coy.

"Yeah, see you, maybe," he said to me and went inside.

"What was all that?" Angie asked again.

"Just Coy being Coy," I said.

"Let's go, I'm hungry," she said and got in the car. She drove us down to Sam's and parked.

"You want something?" she asked.

"I've eaten," I said.

"I'll get something and you can drive us down to the river," she said.

"Are you sure?"

"Sure, I'm sure. I'll be right back."

She went to get her food, and I thought about the drive between Sam's and the river. It was just a few miles, and it would have been a nice, easy drive, if not for the bridge we would have to cross between here and there. It was *the* bridge, Old River Bridge. The one he drove off, and I hadn't seen it or been on it since my father died. I should have told Angie that I didn't want to see it, much less drive across it, but I didn't. I thought she would be disappointed if I wasn't willing to drive her to the river, so I said nothing.

"Let's go," she said, and walked over to the passenger side of the car. "Scoot over. You're driving. Take me to the river." I nodded, but didn't speak as I moved over to the driver's side. I fumbled for the key and started the car. Driving had never been a problem for me. I enjoyed it, and it came easily, but not now. I felt clumsy and self-conscious as I backed out and pulled up to the highway. Angie reached over and turned on the radio to her favorite Memphis station. I moved onto the highway towards the river and the bridge. Suddenly, I really did not want to do any of this. I looked over at her and thought again about some way to get out of it before it was too late. The wind in her hair and the smile on her face told me again that I wouldn't be turning back. We were going to the river, and the only way to get there was to drive across Old River Bridge.

I was breathing hard already, and we were still two or three miles from the spot. Soon, I could hear my heart beating in my ears and feel my hands getting moist on the steering wheel. It was like he was standing outside my bedroom door again, and I had nowhere to run. I drove us around the last corner before the bridge came in sight, and I could feel the car slowing way down, but I didn't feel in control of what was happening. Angie asked me if I was okay. I couldn't answer. I don't think I was aware of what I was doing when we came to a stop at the foot of the bridge. I looked over to the left and down into the water. I pictured him, in his truck, going under the surface. I think I started to cry.

"What's wrong?" she nearly shouted at me.

I couldn't speak. Instead, I slammed my foot down on the accelerator and launched the car onto the bridge. I pushed it to the floor and held it there. The car lurched from side to side as we crossed over. Angie screamed. I don't remember breathing until the bridge was behind us, and I had turned the car onto the shoulder of the road and stopped. She pushed the gearshift into park, turned the car off, and grabbed the keys out of the ignition.

We sat there a few moments before speaking. I was crying for sure now. My eyes were watering, and I could feel the tears crawling down my face. I looked out the window and away from Angie's stare. I didn't want her to see me crying, but I didn't have much choice now. I tried to clear my eyes and face without being too obvious, before turning to face her. I could tell by the look on her face that she didn't know what to say.

"The bridge," I was finally able to say to her. "That was the bridge that…"my voice trailed off.

"Oh my God Neil, I am sorry. I should have known," she said. "I wouldn't have asked you to come out here. I didn't realize this was the place. God, I'm sorry."

"It's okay," I said and turned away from her again. "I had to see it sooner or later." She watched me a few moments before asking, "What do you want to do?"

"You better drive," I said. She nodded and walked around to the driver's side of the car. I slid over as she got in and restarted the car.

"Let's go to the river," she said, smiling now. "You okay with that?"

"Yeah, let's go to the river," I answered, and watched her as she put the car in gear and drove us down toward the Mississippi.

I started to feel better in minutes, watching her. We had the windows down, and the breeze was blowing her hair back. She looked prettier and prettier to me as I studied her face while she drove. She could tell how closely I was watching her, and she seemed to like it. She looked over at me every minute or two and smiled. It was starting to feel like this day was going to be okay after all. I had gotten past my first real test at the radio station, and I had made it over that bridge without killing us.

I felt the river getting closer, followed by the smell.

It smelled muddy and clean at the same time. I looked out across the fields as we drove parallel to the river and saw the top of a towboat churning upstream. Angie pulled the car off the highway and onto a sandy field road that led down to the riverbank. We pulled up beside a row of cottonwood trees and stopped. I had seen the river hundreds of times, but it was always impressive, and I was still drawn to it, despite the family picnic, the bridge, and everything that came with it. It was still by far the most impressive and powerful thing I had ever been close to.

It looked that way today. The sky was clear and it was almost hot, but there was a nice breeze off the river. I couldn't have been in a better spot. And even with all that had happened in the last few weeks, this moment and this place made me feel lucky. I still had no idea what Angie really thought about me or what she had in mind for us. Maybe she didn't know either, but that was all right with me right now and right here.

We got out of the car and walked over to the shade of the stand of cottonwood trees lining the river. Angie brought her food, and we sat there while she ate, watching the river flow by. There was not much need to talk in a spot like this. You could easily just sit and listen to the wind and look out across the water, water that seemed to stretch forever. There was Arkansas way over there on the other side, a whole different place to imagine, a place that we couldn't reach from here. A little ways downstream, the towboat I had seen earlier from the car was making its way towards us at what looked like a walking-speed. The big, shiny, white boat—reaching three stories up off the river—was pushing a string of barges in front of it. The boat could have come all the way from New Orleans, and it might be heading for St. Louis, or onto the Ohio River and Cincinnati, impossible to know which, but also impossible not to try and imagine the places it might end up. Pieces of wood, some the size of tree trunks, floated in the opposite direction the boat was headed. The river and everything in it was moving. It was all going someplace.

Angie finished her hamburger and looked over at me. "I love it here. I think I could watch the river all day," she said.

"Yeah, it's really something. I like it too," I answered.

"I like to think about all the places the river passes, all the towns and all the people. It's like you're connected to those people and those places without having to go to them. I think about other places and other people, a lot. But I want to see those places for myself. I want to live in other places, maybe even faraway places, and get to know the people who live there. I think that would be great. I want to figure out how to do that," she said, and looked at me. "How about you? Are you going to live in Harper's Junction all your life? Do you think about living in other places?"

"I guess I have thought about it, but I don't know how things will work out. Who knows, there might be a good reason to stay here, and there might be a good reason to leave. I don't know. I think there's time to figure that out," I said.

"How much time," she said. "We'll be juniors this year. That's not much time left. We'll be out of high school soon."

"I don't know Angie. It's kinda like I'm starting some things right now. I'm not really thinking about ending stuff," I told her.

She studied me for a few moments.

"What do you think you're starting?" she asked.

I should have looked at her and said something like,

"well I'm starting to get to know you better," but I didn't. Instead I said, "I'm starting at the radio station. That's one thing I'm starting." She didn't answer, but she looked to me like she might be waiting for me to say the other thing. I shouldn't have worried about embarrassing myself, but I did. I hadn't figured out yet that I worried about that kind of thing way too much.

Angie and I kept talking. We talked about other things we might do this summer. I told her about my day at the radio station. She told me about working at the drugstore and about some of the crazy people who came in there. She said there were always people coming in who were confused about their medicine, and that Mr. Geist was always patient with them, and he was the same way with Ben and Coy. He knew they goofed off a lot, but he never really got mad at either one of them. I knew about the goofing off part—they were always looking for distractions—and I wasn't surprised by what she said about Ben's dad not getting mad. I had played on a baseball team he coached, and we always had fun. He was never too serious about it, unlike a lot of the other coaches.

We talked about everything we could think of, and the afternoon was the best afternoon I could remember. It was getting late, and I figured we would have to go soon. At that moment, she looked at me and said, "Know what. We need to go to a concert this summer. We need to go to Memphis and go to a concert. I've always wanted to do that. I'll find one for us to go to," she said and waited for me to react. I didn't even have a driver's license yet, and I wondered if she was saying I should take her, or she would take us.

I shouldn't have worried about any of that. When I hesitated, she said, "Don't you think that would be great?" I got my wits together enough to say yes, but I might not have sounded convincing saying it. She didn't wait for me to say anything else before saying, "I need to get home. Are you ready?" I could have said something like, "I wish we could stay longer," because that's how I felt. But all I said was "okay," and we walked back to the car. Angie got in the driver's side without asking me if I wanted to drive.

We would have to cross the bridge again. I thought about closing my eyes, as we got closer to it. Maybe I could just shut the picture out of my mind. The closer we got the sillier that idea sounded. I was going to look. In fact, I was going to get a closer look, a real close look, at the spot. I was sitting on the passenger side of the car, near the railing where his truck would have left the road, and I would be looking down into the water where he disappeared and drowned.

I was mostly glad to not be driving. My palms were getting sweaty again as we approached the bridge, and I could hear and feel my heart beating faster and harder. I could sense Angie looking over at me as we rounded a corner, and the bridge came into sight. She reached over and squeezed my elbow a little. I tried to look over at her and smile, but I couldn't manage it. I looked out the window and saw the bridge railing and the brown water below it. There were new shiny pieces of metal railing attached to the bridge uprights about a third of the way across. It was where he had gone over the side. I glanced down below to the muddy water, and for a moment the thought hit me that he and his truck might still be down there, that maybe I could jump in and pull him out. Maybe all that had happened could be erased, and he could be alive again. And just as quickly, I thought about how many times I had pictured this, or something like it, as a way out for me and my family. And as that idea passed, I chose instead to leave him there in my mind, to not ever imagine saving him, because I never would have.

Angie and I didn't talk about my father or the bridge anymore as she drove us back into town and dropped me off at the store. It was nearly closing time when I got there. Momma was counting money from the cash register and putting numbers down in the store's ledger when I went in.

"Where have you been?" she asked first thing.

"I went down to the river...with Angie, after I left the radio station," I answered.

"The river, with Angie," she repeated.

"She wanted to go," I explained. "We went in her car." I could tell by the way Momma was looking at me that she knew what that meant so I went ahead and said it. "We drove over the bridge," I said, leaving out the part about me driving.

"You did," she said without emotion.

"I saw where the rail was broken."

"Yeah, I guess you would," she said.

I hadn't thought about it until that moment, but just because I hadn't seen the bridge didn't mean she hadn't.

"Have you been down there?" I asked her. "Have you seen it?"

"Yes," she said, and nothing else.

I looked at her for a while, trying to figure out what she was thinking.

"I thought about jumping in and trying to save him. What if I had been passing by and saw it happen?" I said to Momma. "You think I would have jumped in to try to save him? Think I should have? You think anybody would have? You think you would have?"

She was quiet, but I could see tears forming in her

eyes, and I was immediately sorry for what I said. I started to say something else, but she cut me off.

"Let's go," she said, and she sounded mad all of a sudden. She dropped what she was doing. She didn't finish counting, and she left the ledger on the counter. I started to pick it up, but she stopped me.

"Let's go, right now."

I followed her out to the car, and she drove us over to the house. I got out and started to go inside.

"The garage," she said, and she said it like it was an order.

"What about the garage?" I asked.

"The boxes, put them in the car." I didn't have to ask which boxes, and it sounded like I shouldn't ask why I was putting them in the car. I picked up one of the boxes of my father's stuff and loaded it in her station wagon.

"All of them," she said.

"What are we…"

"Just put them in the car," she said without explanation.

We filled the back of station wagon with boxes. And I looked at her to find out what was next.

"Get in," she ordered.

"Where are we…"

"Just get in," she said.

She backed out of our driveway in a great hurry and sped off down the street. She never drove fast. Now she seemed desperate to get someplace as fast as possible. She drove us up to the square and out to the highway. It was late in the day now, and the sun was starting to set. She drove south from town and turned west onto the river road, picking up speed the whole way. We were heading toward the bridge, and I was scared.

I wasn't used to her driving like this, and she seemed out of control.

I looked over at her. Tears were streaming down her face, and her mouth was moving. She was talking to herself, but I could barely hear any sound coming from her. We got within sight of the bridge and she slammed the steering wheel with her hand. She hit it so hard I was afraid she might have broken her hand. She kept the car going full speed as we got closer. It felt like we were going to take off on the ramp to the bridge. We reached the edge of the bridge, and she hit the brakes. I reached for the dashboard as the car skidded and twisted to a stop. I was barely able to hold myself back from hitting the windshield. We were sitting dead still on the bridge.

Momma got out of the car, walked around and opened the back gate of the station wagon. She grabbed the first box she could reach, walked to the new section of railing on the bridge, and flung it over and into the brown water.

"Son of a Bitch," she screamed, and walked back towards the car. I was still sitting there, stunned. She yelled at me. "Come on. Help me!"

I got out and grabbed a box. Momma got one too, and we walked over to the railing together.

"Son of a Bitch!" I yelled this time as we threw our boxes off the bridge. We were both crying as we ran back and forth to the car to finish the job. When the job was done and the last box disappeared below us, Momma was sobbing, and I guess I was too. She reached over and pulled me in close to her. We hugged and cried for what seemed like a long time. Finally she said, "That's the end of it Neil. You hear me, that's the end of it."

Chapter 10

It felt like there was a lot to do. Summer had always felt easier and slower in the past, but now I had this job to work on. We were going to be moving soon, I needed to get my driver's license, and I was thinking about things that Angie and I could do together, things that she would like. This summer felt different.

My birthday was coming up in a couple of weeks and I needed to study for the driver's test. I also wanted to spend as much time as I could at the radio station, and then take that last big step—talk on the radio. I waited until around noon and walked up to the square. I put my earpiece in, turned my little radio on, and headed for the drugstore. Billy was on the air playing music and talking loudly. He played Neil Young's "Heart of Gold" then said something about "solid gold" and played a Beach Boys song. Whatever he said, it didn't mean much to me. I already knew I wasn't going to try to sound like Billy when I got on the radio. He played a couple of more songs and then went into the local news at noon.

Billy read two stories about the funeral arrangements for people who died recently in Harper's Junction. The stories mentioned the names of relatives that the deceased was survived by and a few details of the person's life. "Mr. Stanford was a life-long member of the First Baptist Church," he read about one of the people who died. I wondered what had been said about my father's life on the radio, if anything.

He finished the stories about funerals and then played a report from Woody Lawson about work that was to begin soon on the new Highway 53. He mentioned the congressman who had helped secure funding for this important project. Billy finished the news with scores from the first week of summer baseball for the kids in Harper's Junction. Hearing him read the story reminded me that this was the first summer when I hadn't played baseball since I was five-years-old, and I realized that was another reason this summer felt so different.

I got to the square about the time Billy was ending his news report. I pulled the earplugs out, tucked them away in my pocket with my little radio, and walked around behind the drugstore to see who was parked back there. Angie's car wasn't there, but Ben's Mustang was. I figured I could kill some time with him until Chris got to work at the station. I thought about going in through the back door of the drugstore where the people who worked there entered, but I decided against it and walked around to the front doors. The delivery truck was parked out front.

"What's going on?" Ben, said, smiling, when I walked in. He was sitting behind the soda fountain reading a magazine.

"Nothing really, I'm going over to the radio station when Chris gets in," I said.

"Yeah, let me check to see if there is anything going out. I want to get out of here." Ben said, and went back to talk to his father. Mr. Geist saw me and called out.

"Neil, good to see you. How have you been?"

"Fine, I'm okay," I answered.

"You been to the radio station?" he asked.

"Going over there later."

"Good, good. So we'll hear you on the radio soon," he said.

"Maybe, I hope so."

"We'll be listening," he said, and went back to work.

"I've got one delivery," Ben said.

Ben walked out to his father's delivery truck, and I followed.

"When is your birthday?" he asked me when we got in.

"The 25th," I answered. "I need to study for the test."

"Yeah, you've got time."

"Hey, have you thought about baseball? I heard something about it on the radio a while ago."

"I have. It's weird, no baseball," he said. "Dad said something about it the other day. I think he's going to miss it." Ben was the only kid I knew who called his father "Dad." Ben's father had coached baseball since coming to Harper's Junction, and he coached Ben before that when they lived in Chicago. "He also said something about Marcus. That's the first time he's said anything about him in a long time."

Marcus was a black kid from St. Louis who came to Harper's Junction to spend the summer with his grandfather when we were thirteen years old. That was also the summer Ben and his family moved here, and Mr. Geist put Marcus on the first baseball team he coached in town. He was the first black kid to ever play in what had been an all-white league before that. Marcus took a lot of crap that summer from some of the other players and from some parents. I found out later that Mr. Geist had taken a lot of heat from people in town.

Marcus didn't make it through the summer. There was trouble with some redneck boys from out in the county, and Marcus got blamed for it. He had to go back home before the season ended, and we never saw him again. Everyone who played on the team with Marcus came to like him and admire the way he played. He was a funny kid with a big personality.

Other black kids came over to play baseball with us the next summer, and it wasn't such a big deal after that. Marcus and Mr. Geist helped make that happen.

Ben drove us out to Jefferson Street towards the park and turned left, crossing the railroad tracks that divided Harper's Junction. The town was pretty much all white on the west side and all black on the east side—the other side of the tracks as people around town called it. You could get some funny looks and even stares driving around the other side if you were white. The people there would want to know what you were up to. There was some mingling of blacks and whites in a few of the businesses in town, and now the schools had integrated, but neighborhoods were one or the other. Of course the churches were segregated, and the two groups didn't socialize with one another, ever.

Folks on the black side of town were used to seeing Mr. Geist's delivery truck. There was no black-owned pharmacy in Harper's Junction, and much of the business from black customers had gone to Mr. Geist since he bought one of the old pharmacies on the square and opened shop. They seemed to like him and trust him. Ben drove past the black grocery store, the café, and the barbershop that stood clustered together at the center of this part of town. Several older black men were seated on benches outside the businesses. They waved to us and Ben waved back.

Ben drove up to a tiny house at the edge of town and stopped. He grabbed the small white paper bag he had brought with him, got out of the truck, and walked towards the broken-down front porch of the home. A screen door swung open before he reached the porch, and an old black woman wearing a faded plain brown dress and house shoes stepped out to greet him. She called him Mr. Geist and thanked him several times for bringing her medicine. Ben was very polite and told her she was welcome and to let him know if she needed anything else. She smiled and waved out at me before stepping back inside the screen door.

"Mrs. Rodgers," Ben said when he got back in the truck. "Nice lady."

"You know her?" I asked.

"Well, I know her from bringing her medicine. That's all," he said. "A lot of times she offers me something to eat when I come out here."

"You ever eat it?"

"No, no. I'm not sure what she might have. You people down here eat some funny stuff," he said. It was something he was comfortable saying to me, but Ben was usually careful about making fun of people in Harper's Junction.

"Yeah city boy," I said. "Us people down here eat just fine. I've seen some stuff on your table that I wouldn't touch."

"You've seen food on my table that you couldn't even pronounce," he said, smiling. And that was true. Ben's mother drove to Memphis about once a week to buy groceries and she came back with stuff I had never seen—kosher foods like special bread, meats, and pickles. I had tried some of it, but I usually stuck to food I could recognize when I ate at Ben's house.

"I need to go by the house. You got a minute?" Ben asked and I nodded. We drove back up Jefferson Street, around one side of the square and out to Main Street. Ben lived on a short, dead-end street less than a mile from the square. There were only a few houses on the street, and they were some of the nicest homes in town. He parked the delivery truck and

I followed him inside. The Geist's had nice things—stuffed furniture, dark wood tables, and brass lamps. They also had a small table just inside the front door with brass candlestick holders and a blue star above that said, "Home Blessing" at the top and below that it said, "May this home be a place of happiness and health, a place of contentment, curiosity and wealth. Let kindness and peace herein abide. Let faith be our protection and guide."

"You want a soda?" Ben asked me as he walked back towards the kitchen. He was the only kid I knew who called coke sodas.

"I'd like a coke if you've got one. I don't know about a soda."

"Here's your Coca-Cola, southern boy," Ben said.

"That's me."

We were alone in the house, so Ben turned on the television in the living room. There was a soap opera, *All My Children*, showing. We had watched for just a minute or two when Ben asked me about going to the river with Angie.

"Who told you that?" I asked him.

"Coy saw you with her behind the store, and he asked her about it," he said.

"Yeah, we went down to the river, no big deal," I said, trying not to talk about it. Ben just smiled.

"Are going to ask her on a date?" he said, getting right to the point.

"I don't know man. I don't even have a driver's license yet."

"Sounds like she wants you to ask her out," Ben said.

"Why do you say that?"

"It just sounds that way."

"Did she say something?" I asked, trying not to sound too interested.

"I don't know what she said, but she's been giving you rides and now the river," he said.

"I think we're just friends," I said. "I don't know what we are."

And I didn't know. We were all just turning sixteen, and the boys were trying to figure this stuff out. The girls were ahead of the game by a long stretch. The older boys had been asking them out since they were freshmen, and they knew more about how to act and what to do on dates. Most of us boys, including me for sure, didn't know much. We knew what we had seen on TV and in the movies. We watched the older kids at school and around town, but that wasn't the same.

In the little time I had spent with Angie, it seemed like she enjoyed being around me. I really didn't know why that was so, and I was very afraid of blowing it with her. There was no study book for that. I was trying to figure out what made her happy and what might make her like me. I guess I could have asked her. I sat and thought about all that for a few minutes while we drank our sodas and pretended to watch the soap opera. Ben finally said that he needed to get back before his dad got upset. Something I couldn't imagine. We drove up to the square and he dropped me off in front of the radio station. It was just after two o'clock and Chris was starting. I climbed the stairs and opened the door to the radio station.

Mrs. Burns was there and so was Barry Owens. He was sitting in the chair across from her desk. He was wearing the jacket with the name Garrett on it again. They were both smoking. I said hello when I came in, and she didn't ask me what I wanted or why I was there. That seemed like a good sign.

"You know Barry, don't you?" she asked me. Barry didn't wait for me to answer.

"You're Lois' boy, right?" he asked.

"Yeah, I am."

"Your momma used to hang out at our house when I was a little fellow. Her and my big sister were buddies. I always thought she was the prettiest girl in town. Sweet too."

He paused for a couple of seconds. When I didn't answer he asked me how she was doing. He said it in a way that I could tell he was talking about what happened to my father. I didn't want to talk about it, so I just said she was okay.

"You tell her I said hello. I'd sure like to see her sometime," he said.

I didn't know what to say to that. I nodded and walked to the control room door. I looked inside and saw Chris staring out the window toward the courthouse. I watched for a little while. He looked distant, like he was thinking of someplace else. I knocked and pushed the control room door open.

"How's it going?" I said. He didn't answer. "Barry Owens is out there. You know him, right. Is he okay? People seem to wonder."

"Hard to say. I like Barry, all right. He's been good to me up here. He doesn't say too much. You gonna do this today?" he asked, changing the subject.

"What do you mean? You mean the whole thing?" I asked.

"It's time. If you want to do this, you need to do it now. I don't know how much longer I'm staying," he explained.

"When, what time?" I asked Chris.

"Whenever you say. I've got local news at five. I'll do

that, but you can do any of the rest of it."

"Let me just go over it in my head a little bit," I said, trying to stall. I was trying not to feel terrified, but I could feel it coming on. Hopefully, I could push the buttons and flip the switches, but I had no idea if I could get words out of my mouth with the microphone on in front of me.

"Tell you what, I'll make a playlist for the three o'clock hour. If you want to do it, you can start then. I'll be around if you need me," he said. I said okay and immediately looked up at the clock. It was ten after two, and if I had the power, I would have put the clock on hold at that moment. Instead, the second hand seemed to be flying around the face of the clock. I looked away for what seemed like a moment and another couple of minutes had passed. At this rate, it would be three o'clock before I had a chance to get my head straight.

Chris wrote down a few song titles and handed the paper back to me. I sat there behind him and tried to imagine this really happening. I was going to play these songs and talk on the radio. I had been practicing saying things that I thought I might use when I finally got on the air, but they all seemed stupid to me now. I needed something to say and I needed to come up with it fast. Nothing worked. I replayed things I had heard Chris say, and things that the DJ's in Memphis said. None of it made sense when I said them silently in my head.

"I'm not sure what I'll say," I finally blurted out to Chris as the clock got closer and closer to three o'clock.

"Don't worry about it," he said sharply. "Write some things down if you need to." He gave me a pen and put some old copy paper on a clipboard and handed me that too. I held the pen and looked at the yellow paper. I wrote down my name and the station's name, thinking that I might not even be able to remember those things when I was live, on-air.

I wrote down things like "WHJ weather" and "right now in Harper's Junction," things that I shouldn't have to write down. I tried to write down little things to say about the music, things that I thought someone else on the station might say. I wished I had thought about all this before, and that I had been making notes before. And at that moment, I was wishing that three o'clock would never get here.

Of course three o'clock did come around—in what seemed like a very short time—and Chris put the news on at the top of the hour. Then he got up and moved around me to the very back of the control room. I was still sitting, and I wasn't sure if my legs would get me out of my chair and into his. It felt like I was shaking, but I wasn't even sure of that. I forced myself to stand and moved around in front of the board. I sat down and looked up at the clock. The time was 3:01, four minutes before I had to say something on the radio.

I put my notes down in front of me and tried to think. I needed something to play, and I still needed something to say after the weather. The weather forecast was taped to a clipboard sitting on top of the board. I read over it quickly and saw that Chris had written the temperature down beside the forecast. There was a thermometer hanging in the shade outside the control room window. I glanced out at it, but the numbers didn't register in my head right away, so I decided to use what Chris had written and not worry about changing it. I was 3:03 and time was moving faster than I ever could have imagined.

I needed music to play. I reached around and grabbed the list that Chris had made for me. Carpenters, "We've Only Just Begun" was the first song on the list. I searched up and down the cart rack that held the music WHJ played the most. I should have remembered that the songs that haven't been played recently were at the top of the rack, but my brain felt like it was locked, so I kept looking up and down, not seeing it. While I was frozen there, an arm and a hand reached around me and pulled a cart from the top of the rack and slammed it into the cart machine. Chris had seen me struggling, and he decided to help. I looked up at him and tried to say thanks, but I don't think that came out of my mouth. It was 3:04. I looked at the weather forecast again and read over it. The second hand on the clock had moved past six, and was racing toward twelve.

"Jingle, jingle, jingle," a voice from behind me said. I needed a jingle to play between the weather and the song, but I wasn't sure if I had time to load one in the cart machine. I threw up my hands, and Chris came through again. He grabbed a cart with a jingle recorded on it and pushed it into the machine next to the one with the song. I didn't even try to say thank you.

The second hand was spinning toward ten now, and Chris reached around to my left side and grabbed the headphones. Less than ten seconds to go and I hadn't even thought about putting them on. He slid them over my ears as I shook my head and fumbled for the microphone switch. I did remember that I would have to turn the microphone on before I tried to talk. That was something.

The second hand slid up to the top, and the sound from the newscast ended. I hadn't heard anything that they said, but the network was quiet now, and I knew I needed to go, to say something, to keep things moving. *The weather*, I reminded myself. Things had suddenly slowed down, stopped really. The second or two hole between the end of the newscast and me trying to read the weather seemed like a very big hole. The first words on the weather forecast were: "Mostly sunny today with a high in the mid 80s." I saw the words just fine, but I realized that my mouth was completely dry and that I wouldn't be able to say any of the words, to even make a sound, until I did something to fix that. I brought some spit up into my mouth and rolled it around a little bit, hoping to get some moisture in my mouth. It didn't help much, and in my mind the silent gap was huge now. It was time to say something, or at least make something happen. I thought about starting the song without saying anything. I knew I could manage that. I thought about it, and the idea kind of calmed me a little. If nothing came out of my mouth, I at least knew what I would do next.

I flipped the microphone switch over to the right and turned up the knob that controlled its volume. The microphone was on, and it was turned up; it was time to jump in.

"WHJ weather," I knew I was saying something because I could hear myself a little in the headphones, but for some reason I repeated myself, louder the second time. "WHJ weather, mostly sunny today with a high in the mid 80s." I paused there for what seemed like a long time, though it probably wasn't all that long. "Mostly clear tonight with a low in the mid 60s." Better I thought and paused again, "And partly cloudy tomorrow with a high in the upper 80s." I paused again and tried to make myself remember what to do next. *Temperature,* I thought. *Say the temperature.* I looked back up to the top of the paper and found the number Chris had written there. "It's eighty-one degrees," I said, and then repeated myself. "It's eighty-one degrees outside." I had no idea why I said it twice, maybe just because I could.

With the weather done I looked over at the cart

machines and thought about what to do next. I knew I should start one of them, but for a moment I couldn't remember which one should go first. I stared at the labels on the carts, but it didn't help. I had to play something. Things had come to a complete stop again, and a new hole of silence was opening up. I reached over toward the green button on the cart machine closest to me and realized that my hand was shaking again. I got my fingers close to the button and kind of poked at it, hoping I would hit it and something would start. It took two tries before something did start, but it was the wrong thing. The song started, not the jingle that I was supposed to play first. I looked over at the other machine and thought about playing the jingle, but I figured it was too late. The song was playing, and I had just a few seconds to say something over the instrumental introduction before the singing started.

I needed to make more words come out of my mouth. *Carpenters*, I thought, *say The Carpenters or say WHJ, just say something.* I could tell the singing was getting real close, and I had maybe a couple of seconds to do something.

"The Carpenters on WHJ!" I said, practically shouting. I was surprised that I said it. I was more surprised that it sounded like I was yelling. I remembered to turn off the microphone. I sat for a few seconds trying to re-focus, thinking about what was next. I remembered Chris was standing behind me, so I turned around to look at him. He was trying not to laugh.

"I guess that could have been worse," he said. I don't think he was trying to be mean about it. He was just trying to be funny and loosen me up. "You'll be ready this time," he added, and pointed towards the music playlist.

I was a little more ready when the record ended, and I

told myself not to shout this time. I put the cart in for the next song and waited. "WHJ with the Carpenters and 'We've Only Just Begun,'" I said as the song faded away. I don't think I said it loud enough that time, since I was trying not to yell. I hit the green button on the cart machine to start the next song and tried to remember what I had planned to say next. "These are the Temptations and 'It Was Just My Imagination.'" All the words came out, and even though my voice was quivering, and I couldn't tell how loudly or softly I was speaking, I had this thing going, and I hadn't passed out or thrown up. I hadn't tried to say anything clever, but I wasn't about to try that in my first hour on the radio.

I clunked along for an hour. I had to stop and play several commercials—they called them spots at the radio station—between songs, and that made things more complicated. I had to pull out carts that had been played and replace them with ones to play next, while thinking about having to talk. There were gaps when I didn't act quickly enough. And I might have played the same spot twice within a minute, but I was okay with it. It seemed like both a short, and a long hour. I was worn out and it had only been an hour.

"You want to do another hour?" Chris asked. He had sat down in the chair behind me and pretty much let me go on my own after my bumpy start.

"Not this time," I was quick to answer. "Next time," I added.

"Yep," he said.

I was staring at the hands of the clock trying to calculate where my record would end and how much time would be left before the top of the hour. I never had to worry about that when Chris was announcing. He could fill the time, no problem. I had a song to announce and the station identification to do before the news started, but it looked like I had at least twenty seconds extra to fill after that. I should have asked Chris what to do.

I was playing Chris' last selection for the hour, "Joy to the World" by Three Dog Night, and I was running out of time and ideas on how to fill time. I don't know why I did it, but here's what I did: The record ended and I said, "That's Three Dog Night with 'Joy to the World' and this is WHJ, Harper's Junction Tennessee. It's eighty-four degrees at four o'clock." Except it wasn't quite four o'clock, and I had nothing else to say. I should have made myself sit quietly for those fifteen seconds and not worry about the dead air, but I couldn't. The title of the song that just ended, "Joy to the World," was still in my head and it made me think of the Christmas carol by the same name. It was the only thing in my head when I announced, "Joy to the World! And Merry Christmas to all!"

I could not believe what had just come out of my mouth. I had panicked and wished the people of Harper's Junction Merry Christmas on June 15th, possibly the stupidest thing ever said on the radio.

I turned off the microphone and slowly turned around to see Chris' reaction. He looked at me and burst out laughing. It was that funny. It might have been funny to me too, if I wasn't overcome by embarrassment, and if I wasn't the one who said it on the radio.

I got up from the announcer's chair in a rush, nodded at Chris, and left the control room. I walked quickly down the hall past Woody's office without looking inside to see if he was back. I passed Mrs. Burn's desk out front without looking at her either. I raced down the steps, out the front door, and onto the sidewalk. I didn't look at anyone, just in case they heard what was just said on the radio and knew that I was the one who had said it, as unlikely as that was.

I left the square and pretty much ran home. I was already hoping to erase the memory of what I had just done, but I also knew that would probably never happen. I wondered if I should even go back to the radio station.

Chapter 11

I tried to sleep as long as I could the next morning. There was no school, and I didn't want to work at the store or even think about going back to the radio station. I woke up replaying the chorus from "Joy to the World" over and over in my head. I had no idea how to shake it. It was almost noon when I got out of bed. The television was on in the living room. Ginny was watching soap operas.

"Mr. Radio Man, I thought you were going to stay in the bed all day," she said. I was already mad thinking about what happened the day before, so I told her to shut up, which was something I almost never said to her, and it hurt her feelings.

"That's not very nice," she said, and she was right. I should have apologized, but I didn't.

"What are you suppose to be doing?" I asked her. We had just started our summer vacation, and we needed to work out a routine. Ginny would have to go to the store or to Nana's house if I wasn't around. Momma wouldn't let her stay home all day by herself.

"Momma told me to come to the store if you left," she said. "Are you leaving?" I told her I was leaving, but I really didn't have anywhere to go. I just needed to get out. I knew that much. Ginny frowned because she wanted to hang around the house all day. There was no television at the store, and she and Nana couldn't agree on what to watch or what to do all day at her house. I couldn't blame her for wanting to stay home, but I didn't want to babysit either. She would probably be able to talk Momma into letting her come home later in the day anyway. Ginny huffed around the house for a while and then left to go to the store.

I scraped up all the money I could find around the house, got my little radio, and walked out the door with no plan. I looked in the garage and saw my bicycle sitting there. It was a funny thing; once some of the kids in my class started getting their driver's licenses we all pretty much stopped riding bicycles, especially around town. I looked at the bike and felt like getting on it, but I didn't. I would have enjoyed being out riding it, but I didn't want to be seen riding a bike by someone my age.

If things went well, I was only two weeks away from getting my driver's license, and maybe I wouldn't have to worry about walking or bike-riding anymore. I walked away from the house and turned away from the direction of the square and in the direction of the park. It was a walk or a bike ride I had taken a lot in the summers since I was old enough to go there by myself. The pool was there and the baseball fields. I had spent as many summer hours as possible at both places, but it seemed like that time was ending. There was no more summer baseball for kids my age, and the pool was mostly for younger kids too. My friends were driving cars and getting jobs. That's what I had in mind too, at least until yesterday. I walked in that direction, thinking about all of that and wondering why I was even going there now. I made my way over to Jefferson Street and turned left toward the park.

The sidewalk was worn and familiar. I had been on it hundreds of times, it seemed. I knew all the houses along the street too, and most of the people who lived in them. I knew the houses where kids lived, and the ones with old people. I knew what most of the fathers who lived in those houses did for a living, where they worked, and what they did when they weren't working. I knew the fathers who hunted and fished, and the ones who coached baseball and did things with their kids. And I knew the ones who didn't do those things—the ones like my father who weren't seen around town very much. I wondered about those fathers, even more now that mine was dead.

I walked and thought, and by the time I reached the park I knew I had no reason to be there. I walked down to the pool and looked out at the little kids splashing around, and the older ones hanging around, lying on their towels, talking loudly, while trying to catch the attention of a boy or girl. Even the older kids I saw were a year or two younger than me. I bought a coke at the concession stand and walked down the hill towards the baseball fields. I sat down at the top the grass-covered bank that bordered the outfield of the larger of the two fields and stared out across them.

The fields would be covered with kids later. The lights would be on, and the boys would be wearing their neat, clean uniforms. The coaches, all of them fathers, would be wearing their team's caps, and the place would be buzzing with parents and grandparents in the stands watching. Little kids, the brothers and sisters of the bigger boys who played, would be running around like crazy, stopping to try and talk their moms into giving them money for the concession stand.

But it was all quiet now, and the field was empty. I sat and pictured myself over at third base, Coy at second, Ben at first, Ben's dad standing in front of the dugout with his Cub's cap on, clapping his hands and shouting encouragement. And of course I imagined Marcus standing just below me in centerfield. He roamed most of the outfield really; he was that good. We had only played part of one season together, but he left a big impression on me, and, I think, on everyone else in the league.

Ben loved the Cubs and so did his dad. He gave us all Cubs nicknames. When I played third I was "Santo" for the Cub's Ron Santo, Coy was "Beck" for Cub's second baseman Glenn Beckert, and of course we had to call Ben "Banks" for Ernie Banks, his favorite Cub ever. Coy hated it since he was a Cardinals fan, and his favorite player had always been their second baseman, Julian Javier. I hadn't thought much about it when the season ended late last summer, that our baseball together was over, but now it was clear and it was sad.

I finished my Coke, pulled out my little radio, and lay back on the grass. I put the earpiece in and clicked it on. I had been listening to my favorite Memphis station earlier, so I tuned over to 1330 and heard that song by America called "Horse with No Name". It was a song that I knew, and the song made no sense to me, but it sounded good and Chris came back with a good line about "naming that horse for these guys" when it ended. I liked what he said, and I liked the way he sounded. Most importantly, I knew what I had to do.

I turned off the radio, put the earpiece back in my pocket, and ran up the hill past the pool and onto Jefferson Street. I walked as quickly as possible back to the square and hurried up the stairs and into the studios at WHJ. I said hello to Mrs. Burns and to Woody who was sitting at his desk, but I didn't slow down to talk to either of them. Chris was about to talk as I waited outside the door of the control room. I watched him flip on the microphone switch as the red "On Air" light came on above him on the wall and just above me over the door. He talked his way easily through the weather and into his first song of the hour, which was "Nice to Be with You". He sounded like a person who felt like it was nice to be with his listeners, whether he was or not.

I opened the door and walked in. Chris turned around and took off his headphones. He was frowning and shaking his head a little.

"Boy this song sucks," he said to me first thing. "You ready to do this again?" I said I was, and thankfully he didn't mention what happened the day before. "Why don't you put together a playlist for the next hour," he said to me. "You need to do as much of this as you can. Mix it up," he said to me about the songs I was choosing to play. "Fast, slow, happy, sad, old, new. Don't just play the ones you like the most either. You have to play all the new songs Woody puts back here, or he won't like it."

I got busy and made a list for three o'clock. I tried to follow what Chris said. I mixed up the music and even scheduled a couple of my least favorite songs. I looked through the record rack for some old songs to play and saw "My Girl" by the Temptations. It was a great song, and I thought about Angie when the lyrics came in my head. Of course, she wasn't my girl, but I imagined what I would say on the radio if she were, and I was playing this record. The thought made me smile. And even though I wouldn't be saying anything about her on the radio today, I pulled the record and put it on my list.

I made notes in the time I had before going on the air. I wrote down intros for the weather, for some of the records I would be playing, and added some things to say about WHJ and about what kind of day it was in Harper's Junction. I wanted to say something about summer, about school being out, and how people were feeling about that. I tried to figure out how to tie that into a couple of the songs on my list. Most of all, I didn't want to leave anything to chance—no more getting caught with nothing to say and embarrassing myself by blabbering about nothing. I was still plenty nervous, but it didn't feel like I couldn't catch my breath, that my mouth was completely dry, or that my palms were wet. I felt a little better as the clock moved towards three o'clock.

The news started, and Chris got up to let me in.

"I'm going to go down the hall for a little while," he said. "Come get me if you need anything." He was going to leave me in here by myself. I wasn't sure that was the best idea, but I didn't argue. I knew he wanted me to do this by myself, that it was the best way to learn. "You'll be fine," he said as he walked out. "Just take it easy, relax." I knew I wouldn't be relaxed, but I also knew what he was saying. It didn't help to freak out about it.

I sat down and got everything lined up: the copy for the weather, the jingle, the song. I even had time to pull the first commercials I would need later in the hour. I took several deep breaths and watched the clock count up to 3:05 *I can do this,* I started saying to myself, and I said it over and over. I kept repeating it until the moment I turned on the microphone and said my first words on the radio since the disaster yesterday. The words came out okay—a great relief.

I got through the weather. I played the jingle. I started the song. I introduced the song. The words I was saying were making sense to me. It wasn't great; it probably wasn't even good, but I was happy with it. I was moving the station into a new hour and there was no disaster to report yet. And it kept going that way. I was pushing the right buttons at pretty much the right times, and it sounded something like radio should sound. The only time I got in trouble was during a thirty second commercial where I caught myself thinking about how well it was going and didn't hear the spot end. It might have taken a second or two to get the next one going. Lesson learned. Pay attention always; try not to let your mind wander.

It went on like that until the top of the hour when I began obsessing over hitting the news at four o'clock. I counted and recounted the time I needed to fill before I started my last song. I wanted to do anything possible to avoid what happened yesterday. I changed the last song on my playlist so it would time out better, and I sat and stared at the clock as the record got closer to the end. The song faded out at about twenty seconds before four o'clock , as I turned on the microphone, already proud of myself for the good timing.

"The Jackson Five with ABC. That's how easy everything should be," I said with some confidence. "This is WHJ, Harper's Junction, Tennessee. It's four clock." I finished just as the second hand reached twelve, and I listened for the news to start at four. One problem: I was so proud of my timing that I didn't hit the switch for the news. Dead silence, and it took me three or four seconds to figure out what was wrong. It gave me a little shiver. I had screwed up the top of the hour again, nothing like yesterday, but still embarrassing. I had the news on by the time Chris popped open the control room door. I was expecting him to say something about what just happened, but he didn't.

"Not bad," he said. "I think you can do this." It meant everything in the world to me when he said it. I can only imagine how big the smile on my face looked in that moment.

I stuck around for another hour and watched Chris get ready to do the local news at five. He put together some state news from the wire along with some local stories Woody had prepared earlier in the day. He made notes and marked through some of the wire copy. He was able to do all that while playing music and keeping his show going. Doing the news would be the next big challenge for me, but I didn't want to worry about that today. I had done an okay hour of radio, not a good hour, but not terrible either. I was happy with that. I left the station feeling that way. I waved at Woody when I passed his office on the way out and he smiled. Mrs. Burns smiled too. Best of all, I was looking forward to coming back.

I practically skipped down the stairs and out onto the square. I looked across the way at the drugstore and walked that way. I watched the front window as I crossed the courthouse lawn, hoping to see Angie inside. The sun was shining from behind me onto the glass, so I couldn't tell who was at the soda fountain, or the counter. I pushed opened the front door and looked for her, but she wasn't there. I'm sure I was frowning when she popped up from behind the counter.

"I didn't see you back there," I blurted out.

"Yeah, I was putting some stuff in the case," she answered and smiled. Her hair was shining from the sun coming through the window, and she was wearing a white shirt with ruffles on the front. I couldn't imagine anything prettier. I must have stared at her for several seconds before I realized I hadn't said anything.

"I was over at the uh, radio station," I told her.

"How was it?"

"Well it was okay, I think. I did an hour."

"What do you mean?" she asked.

"I was on the radio between three and four," I explained.

She wasn't sure what I was talking about. "You, you were 'on' the radio. Did you talk?"

"Yeah, yeah, I talked and everything."

"Was that the first time?" Angie asked.

I didn't want to talk about the day before so I said, "I did a little yesterday, but today I did the whole thing."

Angie smiled again and shook her head.

"Wow Neil, that's great. You were on the radio. Was it fun?"

"I don't know about fun. It was tense. Maybe, it will get fun later."

"Sure it will," she said, and she said it like she was certain of it. "A lot more fun than this," she said, talking about her job. I didn't have anything good to say back about that, and she could tell.

"Let's celebrate," she said. "I'm getting off in about thirty minutes. Let's go down to the river. We'll get something from Sam's and watch the sunset.

"Yeah, sure," I said, and smiled.

"I need to tell Momma where I'm going," she said and walked to the back of the store to use the telephone. I sat down on a stool at the soda fountain and imagined her and me back at the river. I must have been grinning, because all of the sudden I heard someone say, "What are you so happy about? That is one shit-eating grin!" It was Ben. "Bet I can guess," he said. "I just saw her on the phone." I avoided the Angie talk and told Ben where I had been. His tone changed.

"That's really good, you were on the radio by yourself. Tell me next time," he said. "I'd like to hear it."

"I don't think there is much to hear yet, maybe after I practice some more." I wanted to make sure it didn't sound like I was bragging, and I didn't quite believe that what I had done so far was worth listening to. We all grew up listening to radio, and I knew I wasn't even close to what Ben was used to hearing.

"Well, I do want to hear it," he said, and I believed he meant it.

Angie came back to the front and kind of nodded her head at me. I knew that meant that she had told her mother, and it was okay for her to be out late. I also knew that she didn't say it out loud because Ben was standing there.

"You want to do something later?" Ben asked me. I didn't want to lie to him, but I also didn't want to tell him our plans.

"I've got this driver's test coming up. I should probably look at that stuff," I said.

"You want a ride home?" he asked. "I've got a delivery. I'll drop you off."

"Uh, well, Angie is going to give me a ride," I said, trying not to sound too sheepish about misleading him before. Of course, Ben knew what was going on.

"Driver's test," he said and repeated himself. "Driver's test. That's what they call it now. Study hard," he said and walked away grinning.

Angie had a little time left to work. I told her that I would meet her out back later. I left the drugstore and walked over to the bench to wait. The square began to cool and a few more clouds moved in as I sat and waited. I dug around in my pocket to check on my money situation. I had less than a dollar, and it made me feel anxious. We were stopping at Sam's on the way to the river, and I wouldn't be able to pay, again. It would be embarrassing, even when she knew how to make it okay. As much as anything, I wanted to get this job started at the radio station so I could have my own money.

My time waiting on the bench crawled by until finally it was time to walk around back of the drugstore and meet Angie. I was leaning against the hood of her car when she opened the back door. I smiled and she smiled, and I could hardly believe how good I felt getting in the car with her to drive off together.

We turned into Sam's and I fumbled for my pocket again, trying to pretend there might be real money in there. I dug the change out and stared at it, trying to give her a clue about my situation. She glanced over and said, "I got it," without changing expression.

"Sorry, I should start getting paid soon."

"Don't worry about it Neil, really," she said and I didn't say any more about it.

We got the food—a couple of cheeseburgers, fries, and cokes—and she asked me to drive again. I was still nervous about driving without a real license, but I got behind the wheel and drove us out the highway and onto the river road. We crossed the bridge again a few miles down, and I made myself not look down as we passed. Angie watched me as we went across, and I was relieved, maybe a little surprised too, that it didn't affect me much to be there.

I turned off the river road and parked by the row of cottonwood trees again. We sat in the car with the windows rolled down and started to eat. Angie squeezed ketchup from little packages onto the white paper bag the food came in and sat it down between us. I reached over with my French fry at about the same moment she reached down with hers. I looked up at her when I did, and she was grinning, a big grin, and it made me as happy as anything I could remember.

We finished eating, and Angie got out of the car and walked down to the riverbank. She climbed down on some rocks and sat very close to the water. I watched from the bank above until she turned around and motioned for me to come sit beside her. I sat down close to her, but not too close, because I didn't want to do the wrong thing. We sat without talking and watched the river roll by. More clouds were moving in above us, and the breeze was picking up. The wind blew Angie's hair back away from her face as I looked over at her and focused on her soft blue eyes. She could tell I was staring at her, and without looking at me, reached over and touched my arm. We sat like that for a good long while before she took her hand away. I looked at her and wished I had reacted.

"I love the river," she said, breaking the silence and changing the moment. "I don't know why, but I do. Why do you think that is?" she asked me.

"The river is beautiful," I said, trying to sound like I had thought about it before.

"Yeah, it is," she said, "but it's not just that."

"What else?" I asked.

"Maybe, where it's going and where it's been," she answered. "I'm not sure."

"What about where it is now?" I asked.

"It doesn't stay in one place. Not here, not anywhere. That could be what I like it about, what I love about it," she said.

I didn't say anything to that, because I loved where the river was right now and where we were right now. And if I had the power, I would have frozen this moment in time.

We got quiet again and watched the sun drop across

the river. Birds were dipping down into the water as the light faded, and the sky turned pink and blue. We didn't have to say anything about how beautiful it was. I thought about holding Angie's hand, but I sensed that the time for that had passed.

The sun dropped below the trees, and it began to get dark quickly. I could see flashes of light behind the clouds across the water. There was lightning in the distance, and it looked like a storm was coming.

"Maybe we should get going," I said.

"Let's wait a minute," she answered.

The lightning picked up and moved closer to the far bank of the river. It was quite a show—bright flashes of light, silhouetting tall gray and red clouds that were still catching light up high from sun that had set from our view. The thunder followed, and I knew it was time to go. I started to get up.

"Not yet," Angie said, so I stood there beside her and waited while the wind started to pick up. I could see the trees across the river bending when the lightning flashed, and it wasn't long before the flashes also revealed the rain blowing in sheets on top of the water.

"We better go!" I said, almost shouting now.

Angie didn't answer, but she did get up and start to climb the rocks toward the top of the bank. I followed along behind her. It looked like we might make it to the car before the rain hit, but we didn't. A big gust of wind blew a wall of rain on us. Angie ran and I ran; she laughed and I laughed. We were soaked in seconds. She got in the driver's side of the car, and I went around to the other side. She was already in her seat when I got in. Her white shirt was plastered to her body, and she took no notice of it. Her hair was wet and her face was shining from the water running down. It's a picture

I would always remember, and if I hadn't been an insecure fifteen-year-old boy, I surely would have tried to kiss her.

It didn't happen. I didn't kiss her, and the moment passed. I was instantly disappointed in myself, but there was nothing I could do about it now. Angie looked at me and smiled slightly—a smile that hinted she was disappointed too, and that I should have done something. I could have at least said something. I should have, but I couldn't find the words. She started the car, and we drove away from the river in a heavy rain. I kept glancing over at her as she drove, trying not to stare. Her hair was still stuck to the side of her face and her blouse was still stuck to her skin. I wished I were older, or smarter, or at least more confident in myself. And I wondered if I ever would be.

Chapter 12

I had just a few days before the driver's test, and I didn't know how long I had before Chris might quit the radio station. It felt like he was closer to leaving. He wanted me to do more of his hours on the air, and that part was good. It helped, and I hoped I would be able to take over his job soon enough, but I didn't know how Woody felt. He was being friendly to me, and he had said things like, "It's coming along," but it was hard to judge exactly what that meant, and I didn't take it to mean that he thought I was ready, or even right, for the job yet.

And I was waiting until I had my license and a car before I tried to plan something with Angie. That would be a while though, and I didn't want her to think I was not interested in going to a concert together.

I stopped by the grocery store to see my mother, before walking up to the square. Ginny had gone in with Momma earlier, and Nana was there too. Ginny was sitting outside on some empty wooden cases that were stacked alongside the store when I got there, and she didn't look very happy.

"I hate sitting around here all day," she said when she saw me.

"Yeah," I answered. "You could help out more."

"I do, but I don't want to be here all day. I hate it."

"Yeah, you said that."

"Would you talk to Momma? I want to go to the pool," she said, and she sounded pitiful.

"I'll say something, but I don't think it will matter."

Momma was inside moving some things around in the meat case. Nana was sitting in the big chair behind the counter.

"There's the birthday boy now," Nana said.

"Not just yet, I'm ready though," I said.

"I bet you are. How about your license? You have to take a test right?" she asked.

"I do, and I've been studying some. Ben and Coy have taken it, and they didn't have any trouble. I think it will be okay."

"Sixteen," she said and repeated herself. "Sixteen, that hardly seems possible. It seems like your mother should still be sixteen. Where does it go... where does it go?" she wondered out loud. For me, it seemed like time was standing still with my birthday now a week away. Momma heard us talking.

"I'm a long, long, way from sixteen," she said to her mother.

"Maybe in your head," Nana said, "but not in my mine. Seems like yesterday to me, and it seems like Neil was born shortly after that."

"Well, that part is pretty much true," Momma, said to her. "I was just a child when he was born, not much older than he is now."

"You know Ginny wants to go to the pool," I said, in part to change the subject.

"Of course I know," Momma answered sharply. "I want her to help me more too."

"I told her that. Maybe you can do both. Tell her if she'll help more she can go to the pool more. That way she won't be moping around here all day," I said, trying to sound reasonable.

"Well, don't you sound grown up all of a sudden," Momma said, and she even smiled a little. I knew she would let Ginny go swimming one way or the other. Ginny had taken

Daddy's death the hardest, and Momma wanted her to be happy.

I stepped around behind the meat counter and made myself a sandwich, pulled a coke from the drink box, and sat down next to Nana to eat. She smiled and patted me on the back.

"You'll have to clean your granddaddy's car up a little before you start using it," she said to me. "It's been sitting around a while now, and it could use a good cleaning and waxing."

"I can do that for sure," I said, trying not to leave any doubt that I would take care of the car.

"You know I didn't drive when I was your age. Your granddaddy taught me after we married. Not many young girls did," she said. "There wasn't much use for it. We didn't have cars to drive anyway. I really didn't think about it much. Well, maybe I thought about it some. Hard to say what I would have done if I had a car when I was your age," she said.

"I've gotta go," I told them when I finished eating. "I'm going to the radio station, and I might end up going somewhere with Ben and Coy later."

"Stay here for a few minutes please. I'm going to drop Ginny by the pool while you're here," Momma said to me.

"Okay, sure," I answered, and walked outside to speak to Ginny.

"You owe me," I told her. "Momma's gonna take you to the pool."

"I don't owe you squat!" she shot back. I laughed at her, and she almost laughed back. It was a good sign.

The two of them left. I walked back inside and sat down on the stool behind the counter near Nana. With just the two of us there, it hit me that I might ask her about the letter to my father that I had seen, and about the girl who wrote it. There was a chance she knew something, and I could find out more without having to bring it up to Momma.

"Nana do you know anything about a woman named Betty who knew Daddy?" I asked, not wanting to say more if she didn't know.

"Betty, why are you asking about Betty?" she answered.

"So you do know who she was?"

"I might. There was a Betty. She and your Aunt Bobby were friends, and she liked your father at one time, but that was a long time ago. What about it?" she asked again.

"I found a letter from her when he was in the Army. It sounded like they were suppose to get married," I said.

"Well they didn't," Nana said sharply. "I believe she married while he was gone to the Army."

"You mean she didn't wait for him?" I asked.

"I believe that's right."

Momma got back, and I left for the square. I brought my little radio, but I didn't turn it on. I was too occupied thinking about things to want to listen to the radio. How important was the breakup with this girl called Betty and what did it do to my father? Would he have been the same person, the same husband, the same father, if he had wound up with her? Could it be that he would have been different, or not different at all? Maybe he and Momma were just not right for each other, or maybe he wasn't right for anyone.

And I was hoping that this would be one of the last days I had to walk to work. I imagined driving to work, driving Angie around, and meeting the guys whenever and wherever I wanted. It seemed like a perfect thing that was going to happen soon. It was something most kids thought about for years before it happened, and it was about to happen to me.

I had some time before Chris got to the radio station, so I walked over to the drug store and went in. I didn't see Angie, but I saw Coy arranging magazines. I walked back towards him, checking between the aisles in case Angie might be around somewhere.

"Lose somebody?" Coy asked when he saw me looking around. I started to answer, but Coy went ahead and answered his own question.

"She's not working today," he said.

"I wasn't just looking for her," I answered.

"Kind of looked like you were," he said and grinned.

"Let's do something tonight," I said. "Can you get out?"

"Sure, I'll tell Ben," he said. "I'm off at six. You want me to pick you up?"

"I'll meet you here," I said and headed for the door. Mr. Geist saw me from behind the pharmacy stand and called out.

"Neil, how are you son?"

"Fine sir, I'm doing alright," I answered.

"And what about the radio station?"

"I'm going there now," I said.

"We'll be listening," he said, smiling. I said thanks and waved as I left.

I took a seat on a bench in my favorite shady spot on the courthouse lawn and pulled out my little radio. I plugged in the earpiece and listened to the tiny speaker pushing out a song called "Take Me Home Country Roads" that Billy was playing on WHJ. It sounded pretty country to me, and I wasn't interested. I tuned the radio down from 1330 and across several country stations, without stopping very long at any of them. I hit 1070 and stopped to listen to WDIA out of Memphis playing a song I didn't recognize. WDIA was the black station that played a lot of music you couldn't hear anywhere else on the radio. The DJ's were different too. They said things in ways the guys on the white stations didn't.

I kept spinning the tuner down until I got to 680 and stopped again on WMPS—one of the two big rock-and-roll stations in Memphis. A man with a big booming voice was on the air talking about a huge concert coming up soon with Three Dog Night, Black Oak Arkansas and Buddy Miles at the Liberty Bowl football stadium. He said it would be the first concert ever held there, and it was going to be the biggest thing to hit Memphis since Elvis. The show was the week of my birthday, and the idea of it sent my mind racing. Could I get tickets? Could I get Angie to go? Should I even think about it? It fit perfectly into what Angie had said about wanting to go places and see things, like a concert. I was pretty sure she would want to go; I hoped she still wanted to go with me.

Two o'clock passed, and I walked over to the radio station and climbed the stairs to the entrance. Mrs. Burns said hello, but she didn't smile at me the way she did before. It looked like she and I were settling into a normal relationship. Maybe she had stopped thinking about my father's death every time she saw me. I liked that. Woody was in the production room. He waved me in when he saw me.

"Chris said he wanted you to do the news afternoon," he said to me. "You want to do that?" I nodded yes. "Well, take your time with that. Don't get in a hurry. If you feel yourself speeding up, just slow it down and read all the words clearly," he cautioned me.

"Okay, I got it," I said, but I really didn't have it. Him just talking to me about it let me know how important he thought it was, and it scared me a little.

"You'll do fine," he said, and turned around to face the microphone.

I glanced in and saw Chris with his headphones off, before going inside the control room.

"Woody talk to you about doing the news?" he asked when I walked in.

"Yeah, he said it was okay…told me not to read too fast," I answered.

"I've got two or three stories here from earlier that you can use, and we'll check the wire again before five. You can start at three and go through the news at five if you want to. You've got to do the news sooner or later. Sooner's better. I won't be here much longer," he said. It was the first time he had said it just that way, and it sounded to me like he was going to leave the first chance he got.

"I'll do that," I said.

"Why don't you pick your own music then," he told me.

Chris didn't write his down. He grabbed it on the fly, and it always seemed to turn out well, but writing out a list would give me one less thing to worry about. I got a piece of old news copy from the trash and used the blank side to list the songs I would play in the next hour. I remembered what Chris said before about not playing just the songs I liked, but it was hard to write down the songs I didn't like, and there were several that WHJ was playing that I didn't. I wrote some of them down anyway. One of them was a song called "Daddy Don't You Walk So Fast." I had never heard Chris play it. The song was awful, and the fact that it was about a daddy made it even worse.

"Don't forget about some old stuff," Chris said. "About three to one." He was telling me that we played one older song for every three new songs. The oldies were shelved alphabetically in the back of the control room. I turned my chair around and began to look for some songs to play. I pulled "Help" by the Beatles out first, then "Red Rubber Ball" by the Cyrkle. That was a song that played over and over on the jukebox at the swimming pool when I was ten-years-old. Then there was "The Letter" by the Boxtops. It seemed like that was one summer later—another great pool song. Then I remembered "Hot Fun in the Summer Time" from the summer I turned thirteen. It hit me how much fun picking music could be. And I could be a little creative, and maybe play some music that I really liked, music that meant something to me. I was looking forward to getting the songs on the air, and I liked that feeling.

Chris looked at my playlist and smiled a little. "Some summer oldies," he said. "Not bad. A lot of people like 'em."

"Swimming pool music," I said.

"Right."

Chris moved out at three o'clock, and I settled in to do an hour playing my music selections. It was the least nervous I had felt so far. The news ended, and I announced the weather with no trouble, hit the jingle, and started my first song.

"WHJ with some hot fun in the summertime. I'm Neil Robinson and with Sly and Family Stone and more great summer songs coming up this hour on WHJ!"

I said it without pause, and I felt good about it. The rest of the hour went okay too. My talk was okay, although I couldn't come up with any good variations on the summer theme. I introduced my oldies with "from the summer of 1966" and kept going. The music sounded good to me, and it was fun to get the songs on the air.

The hour passed quickly, and I told Chris I wanted to keep going. He said he would help me get some local news stories together to use at five o'clock. I looked for some more summer songs to play and got ready for my second hour. I felt more confident, and the first few minutes of my second hour went well, but I didn't realize I was starting to let my mind wander. I began to imagine what Angie would think if she were hearing this, what my friends would think, even what my father would have thought. I imagined them all being impressed, and I got deeper and deeper into those thoughts while a song was running out, and I had nothing to play next.

I began a frantic search for the commercial I needed to play next. I looked down at the log and over to cart rack, but I couldn't make the connection in my head because I was panicked. I needed to turn on the microphone, but I hadn't found the right cart. There was no way I could talk and find something to play at the same time. I took a chance and grabbed the first cart I could reach, and slammed it into the machine. I turned on the microphone and said something, I'm not sure what, and started the cart. What I played was a commercial for a furniture store's "Big Memorial Day Sale," a sale that had ended three weeks before. I got a cold chill hearing it. I didn't have any idea how bad a mistake this was, but it scared me. I scrambled to get the right commercials lined up to play and was able to get back on track after the mess-up.

Chris pushed the control room door open when I got my next song started. "You pull the wrong cart?" he asked me about the mistake I made.

"I guess so," I answered, without telling him I had really been caught with my pants down.

"Careful, that stuff will bite you. That wasn't too bad of a mistake, but it could have been worse."

I was relieved to hear him say that and it helped snap me back to attention. Keeping this thing going wasn't impossible, but I had to stay focused. That was the big thing—there were no time outs for daydreaming or anything else.

The hour moved along well after that. I tried to spend time reading over the news stories while keeping a close eye on running the board and making sure I was ready for what came next. Since Chris had stepped out, I was able to read my stories out loud. I imagined anyone hearing me would have laughed. I tried talking louder and softer, and with a deeper voice, and with what I thought was a more serious voice. Problem was, I couldn't settle on a style to use. I was getting close to the five o'clock newscast, and not being able to settle on a sound was unnerving me. The nervousness I had felt the first time I talked on the radio was creeping back in. I tried to convince myself to just talk like I had been, but I felt like I needed to sound different reading the news. I was breathing fast again, and my palms were sweaty when I turned on the microphone to start my first newscast.

"Good afternoon it's five minutes after five o'clock, I'm Neil Robinson with local news from WHJ." It sounded to me like I had blurted it out, and that's not the way I wanted to start. WHJ always started the local news with obituaries. There was no daily newspaper in town, and the radio station was the place a lot of people heard about local deaths. The announcement was simple, and I had read over this one several times before the newscast.

"WHJ regrets to announce the death of Leonard Thompson, age eighty-one, of Harper's Junction," I started reading live on the air in a voice that didn't sound much like my own. I began with a low voice that got higher as I got to the man's name. In those few seconds, I didn't know where I was going or what I was saying, because I was listening to the sound of my voice and not hearing the words.

"Mr. Thompson died at his home Thursday," I said, and now I was rushing. I hurried up, I think, to try and get past the bad news. There's a good chance that no one listening could understand what I was saying. I sped through the information about the visitation and the funeral. When I finished the obituary, I stopped and paused for a good five seconds, which gave me time to realize how fast I had been reading. I took a couple of deep breaths and tried to make myself slow down.

The next story was a follow-up to the one I heard before about the new bypass being built on the west side of town. The story said the road would take traffic from highway fifty-three and away from the square, making travel easier for people and big trucks passing through, while making the square safer and more convenient for people who lived in town. Work was scheduled to start soon, the story said, and should be completed in two years. I read the story very slowly and paused every phrase or two for effect. I could now hear myself trying to explain the story as if I was now talking to a young child, maybe even reading a bedtime story. It must have sounded ridiculous to the grown people listening to WHJ. The story was not very long, but it felt like it went on and on. I wanted it to end, so I could stop talking that way.

That story did finally end, and I moved on to a story about the garden club and the roses program that would be presented at the Harper's Junction Library. A woman named Elsie Spivey would be leading the presentation, which would focus on summer care of rose beds. About halfway through the story I realized I had changed my tone again. My pace was somewhere in the middle between the first and second stories, and I was trying to sound like my biology teacher all of a sudden. He liked flowers and liked talking about them in class. I didn't sound like him, but in trying to sound like him I sounded like another, different person.

There were a couple of more stories about meeting notices and then a listing of people who had been admitted to the hospital, as well as those who had been dismissed from the hospital. I tried to sound serious when I said the name of those going in the hospital and to sound happy when reading the names of those going home.

I went from there to weather and finally got out after about five minutes. It felt like it took forever, and I was shaken by what had happened, and how badly I felt like I had performed. Chris came back in the control room and didn't say anything, which told me that I was right about what I had just done and how it sounded. I got up from the board and moved to the back of the control room. Chris sat down and took over. I stood there for a minute or two before leaving. I said goodbye and Chris said, "Yeah, see ya," and that was all. Woody was in his office, and he called me in from the hallway as I passed by.

"Neil, come on in," he said in a friendly way. "I heard the local news. We're going to need to work on that. I want you to record yourself reading the news and listen back to it.

Do it a lot. Practice, over and over, and you'll get better. It's like anything else, like baseball. You played baseball, right? You have to practice to get better. You can come up here and use the production room when nobody's in there, or you could use a portable tape recorder." I was nodding and trying not to look too hurt by what he was saying. "We've got one here you can borrow," he said, and rolled his chair over to an old file cabinet in the corner of his office. He pulled out a cassette tape recorder, a microphone, and a cord. "Here," he said, and handed the equipment to me. "Be careful with it, and grab some wire copy to practice with," he told me.

I should have said something to Woody about working hard or practicing hard, but I didn't. I left the station wondering how bad I had sounded. I knew it was bad, but I could only guess how bad. Mostly I wanted to know if he thought I still had a chance, and how today would figure into me getting on the air regularly, and getting paid for it.

I had the tape recorder under my arm and a wad of news copy in my back pocket as I walked down the stairs and out onto the square. I looked across at the drugstore and thought about going over there, but then I remembered what Mr. Geist had said about listening, and decided against it. If he had listened, I didn't want to talk to him about it. Worse still, if Ben or Coy, or Angie had heard it. I had told Ben I would meet him at the drugstore, but I didn't want to face up to what had happened, so I started to walk home instead.

As I walked I tried to convince myself that this was just a first-time thing that I could get past. Woody was right; I needed to practice. I also needed to not feel sorry for myself. I had gotten better announcing the music on WHJ. I could get better at this too. I had to believe that. I was anxious to look more closely at the tape recorder and give it a try, so I crossed over one street to the elementary school and walked onto the playground behind the school. It was empty, as I hoped it would be, so I sat down on a bench the teachers used for watching the kids and put the tape recorder on my lap. I attached the microphone to the cord, plugged it in, and hit the record button. There was a little window on the front of the machine with a red needle that moved when you talked in the microphone. I pulled the news copy out from my pocket and hit the red record button on the machine.

"Hello, hello, hello," I said quietly into the microphone and looked around to make sure no one was nearby. The needle moved, so I held the microphone in my left hand and raised the copy up to eye level with my right hand and started to read out loud. I tried the low, serious voice, and then I read with a higher voice, like I was explaining something to children. And, finally, I tried to sound as plain as I could. I stopped the machine and looked around again to check if anyone was around, before rewinding the tape and hitting the play button. What I heard was disappointing. The low voice sounded silly, like I was trying to sound like someone else. The second voice sounded even sillier; it reminded me of my kindergarten teacher. The third try sounded more sincere, but it didn't sound good. I knew right away that I needed to sound more energetic and more confident, without sounding phony.

I kept trying. I read the stories out loud and recorded them, listening back to what I had done. I did it over and over, and by the time I stopped, I liked what I was hearing a little better. It was what I needed to do to get better—practice, a lot of practice.

It was starting to get dark, so I turned the tape recorder

off and walked toward the house. I stopped at the edge of the schoolyard and turned around to look at the front of the building. I had been in and out of it hundreds of times. My mother had walked here with me many mornings when I was little. I had played with my friends here for years, both during and after school. Now I was done with the place and Ginny was too. She would be going to a different school in fall. I hadn't been to the school in several years, but I had never really thought about it as something that had come to an end. I was thinking that now, and I believe it had to do with my father dying and me realizing that we would be moving out of our house soon.

My mother was making dinner when I got home. Ginny was watching *The Brady Bunch* on television.

"Radio boy!" Ginny said when she saw me. I didn't answer.

"We heard you today at the store. Momma had the radio on." I waited for her to say something smart-alecky about it. She didn't, but she did chuckle a little bit. Momma heard her from the kitchen.

"He was fine, Ginny," she said. "Neil was good on the radio."

I didn't want to ask, but I did.

"Did you hear me read the news?"

"I did hear it," she answered.

"Well?"

"You'll get better," she said. "You're just starting. You're not supposed to have it all figured out yet," she added, and turned to me smiling.

"I sucked," I said, surprised by what came out of my mouth.

"Neil!" Momma scolded me.

"He's right," Ginny said. "He sucked saying the news."

"That's enough," Momma said. "Nobody sucked and stop saying it."

I could see her mouth starting to turn up around the edges, and I knew she wanted to smile. She thought it was funny—Ginny and I saying "sucked"—but she didn't want to admit it. I kept looking back and forth at the two of them, and I finally burst out laughing. It did suck, and it was funny. They thought so too, and started laughing with me. It took my mother several moments before she could say, "I'm sorry Neil. You know I'm not laughing at you."

I said it was okay, and the three of us sat down to eat. I told her and Ginny about the tape recorder and how I had been practicing. Momma thought it was a good idea. Ginny thought it was kind of weird. I expected her to say something like that. We had just about finished eating when a truck pulled up in the driveway. It was Coy. I didn't come back to the drugstore like I said I would, and he was coming by to find out what happened. I told Momma I was going out with him, and she reminded me not to be out too late.

"Where did you go?" Coy asked when I got in the truck. "I waited on you until after the store closed."

"Sorry, I had something I had to do," I answered.

"Is Ben coming?" I asked, trying to change the subject.

"He said he would be out…he'd catch up to us."

Coy turned his old truck toward downtown, and we circled the square. It was past seven o'clock and all the stores were closed. The only building with lights on was the police station. We left the square and stopped at the Gulf Station on the highway, the only place in town to get gas after dark. Coy's truck rolled over the rubber cord stretched out in front of the gas pumps, and it triggered the bell attached to the building. A very small black man dressed in a Gulf uniform came out to pump our gas. Everybody in town knew him and called him Shorty. Even kids called him that. He was almost always happy, and he seemed glad to see you.

He came over to the driver's window and greeted Coy with, "Yes sir, what can we do for you?"

"Three dollars' worth, Shorty," Coy answered.

"Yes sir," he replied and cranked the handle on the gas pump. He started the pump and then grabbed a wooden box he used to step up on to clean customers' windshields. He stepped up on the box and carefully cleaned the driver's side with a squeegee and a rag that he pulled from his back pocket. He stepped down from the box and reached over to stop the gasoline pump at three dollars. He then carried the box around to my side and cleaned the rest of the windshield. Satisfied with his work, he sat the box down by the pump.

"Check the oil?" he asked Coy. Coy told him he was good and handed Shorty the money for the gasoline.

"Thank you sir," Shorty said. "You boys have a good night, and be careful."

"Will do," Coy answered.

We circled the town a few times—the Dairy Queen, Sam's, the high school, the square—keeping an eye out for Ben's Mustang. I was also hoping to see Angie's Chevrolet. A lot of kids were out. Summer was in full swing, and we were already restless, looking for something to do to make this time seem special. Coy finally pulled into Sam's and stopped his truck into a spot alongside a couple of dozen cars already parked. We sat on the tailgate and watched the cars parade around, waving at the people we always waved at.

"We've got to do something besides just sitting here," Coy said after a few minutes. "I thought we'd see Ben by now."

There were a few kids huddled up a couple of cars down from us. Coy got up and walked over to them. He talked with a couple of them for a little bit and came back.

"They're going out to dump," he said and looked over at me. "Let's go."

"What about Ben?" I asked.

"He'll figure it out," Coy answered.

The dump was actually a field behind the dump. Some of the older kids, including most of the senior football players gathered there out of sight from town to hang out and drink beer. I had never been out there at night when the seniors were around, and I don't think Coy had been either. Neither of us knew anything about drinking beer either. I wasn't sure at all about going out there, but I was curious too.

Coy drove his truck out through the black side of town, past the city limits, and turned onto a gravel road that ran out to the dump. We circled past the dumpsite and rode a little ways on a dirt road to an open field where several cars were already parked. Someone yelled at us to turn off our lights.

"Don't come in here with your lights on," the boy admonished us as he walked over. It was Charlie Walker, a senior football player, who had just graduated.

"Sorry," Coy said. "I forgot." He said it like he had been here before. Charlie shook his head and walked away. I looked at Coy and shrugged. We sat and let our eyes adjust to the darkness. The cars and trucks had made a circle of sorts, and the kids were sitting on the hoods. Girls were draped over boys, and it looked like pretty much everyone had a beer. I looked over at Coy again and shook my head. He knew I was feeling uncomfortable. "Come on," he said and got out. I watched him walk toward the group of people and knew I didn't have any choice. I had to get out.

I walked slowly behind him for a few steps, hoping that he would deflect any grief we might soon be getting from the older kids. The boys were all seniors. The girls they had brought with them were mostly younger. They saw Coy first, and one of them wasted no time in commenting.

"Well, well, the sophomores are here. How about that? You boys bring the beer?"

I figured he was teasing us, but I wasn't sure. Coy answered.

"Uh, no, we couldn't get… no, we don't," he said, struggling for something to say that didn't sound completely stupid. They all laughed anyway.

"Who's got a beer for the sophomores?" Charlie asked the bunch. One of the boys walked around to the back of his truck and pulled out a couple of cans of Pabst Blue Ribbon and tossed them in our direction. We were lucky to catch them. I held my mine and tried not to stare at it. Coy pulled the top on his like he knew what he was doing. He looked at me and nodded, a signal for me to do the same. I pulled the top and let out a long sigh. I watched Coy and waited for him to make the next move. He brought the can to his lips and tipped it up. The beer came pouring out into his mouth, and he caught the foul taste. He tried to stop himself before he got too much in his mouth, and the beer came squirting out the sides of his lips. The older boys cackled.

"Been drinking long?" one of them asked, laughing.

Coy didn't bother answering. He wiped his mouth with the back of his hand and took another drink, a small sip this time. I watched him and wished I were someplace else. If we were going to learn to drink beer, I knew it shouldn't be here, in front of these guys. I felt like I had no choice though, I had to drink the stuff, at least some of it.

"What about you Miss Robinson?" one of them asked, calling me out. I didn't say anything. I took a tiny sip, trying to avoid Coy's mistake, and let the beer sit in my mouth. It tasted awful—a taste I couldn't compare to anything. I knew something about why people drank the stuff, of course, but I couldn't imagine drinking a lot of it. It was foul.

Coy kept drinking, while I mostly held my beer by my side. I was hoping to find a way to get rid of the rest of it. I would have to be sneaky about it. The older boys would have gone crazy making fun of me if they thought I couldn't finish it. I waited for Coy to finish. When I thought he was getting close, I said something to him quietly about meeting Ben. He tried to shrug me off, so I said it out loud so the others could hear.

"We told him we would look for him, and he's not here," I said, louder than was necessary. "We've got to go meet somebody," I said in the direction of the older kids. It didn't matter because they weren't paying attention. Coy tried to save face by shouting out, "We'll bring some more beer back." A couple of them laughed, and one said "right."

I was still holding my beer when we got in the truck. Coy left the headlights off and drove out to the road. I started to the throw the can out the window. Coy tried to stop me.

"Hey, don't do that," he said.

"I'm not drinking that shit," I answered.

"Give it to me then."

"I'm not giving it to you. You're driving," I said, suddenly feeling judgmental about Coy drinking beer while driving. "How do you feel anyway?" I asked him.

"Just a little funny," he answered. "I don't think I'm drunk."

"You don't sound drunk," I said. "One beer, you're probably all right," I concluded, trying to sound like I knew what I was talking about. Coy frowned when I threw the can out of the window.

We drove back towards town, passing a little store on the edge of Harper's Junction that was run by a black man everybody called Boonie. He had been one of the first black policemen in town, and he now had the reputation of selling beer and bootleg liquor to white kids, or anyone else with enough courage to go in his place. I was surprised to see Barry's hot rod parked out front. I mentioned it to Coy.

"That's Barry's car. Wonder what he's doing here."

"Maybe he knows Boonie, or maybe he's just buying beer," Coy said. "We could get beer here."

"We're not getting beer here; we're not getting beer anywhere." I said.

"Chicken shit," Coy said to me.

"Maybe so, dumbass," I answered.

"I'm gonna do it," he said.

"You can do it later. I'm not going in there, and I'm not going back to the dump."

"You can wait in the truck. I don't care."

"Just take me home. You can do what you want to do," I told Coy. He didn't answer, but he did drive on past the place. We were all sixteen-years-old, or close to it, and I knew

183

that most of us were going to try drinking. I wasn't ready for it though. My father's drinking and driving off a bridge while he was surely drunk had made me very cautious of the whole thing. I didn't want to see Coy do it either. The idea bothered me, and scared me too.

He didn't say anything else on the way back to town, and I could tell he was disappointed. He drove around the square and back out to Sam's. We circled the place once and didn't see Ben.

"You gonna stop?" I asked Coy.

"I don't think so. I think I'm done," he said, and drove me home without talking. I didn't say anything either, even when I got out of his truck at my house. I went inside and walked straight to my room without talking to my mother. I thought about the few sips of beer I had and wondered if she could smell it on me if I got too close. I wondered too if Coy was going back out to Boonies, and maybe to the dump.

I got my little radio out and plugged in the earpiece. It was late enough so I could hear some radio stations from far off. Chris had explained a little bit to me about the big clear channel stations that came through after the smaller stations signed off at sunset. He told me about WLS radio from Chicago and said I should listen to their DJ's. He thought they were the best. I tuned the radio down to around nine on the dial and fished around for a signal from WLS. I stopped on some music—a song that I didn't recognize—and listened.

There was a long section of guitar playing. It didn't sound like anything we played on WHJ. The song began to fade, and a rapid-fire announcer came on to talk about it.

"Derek AND the Dominoes!" he said, and then lowered his voice to a whisper. "Careful we don't topple these guys over. One goes—they all go. Oh, what the heck, Layla knocking them down!" he said and then shouted, "I am John Landecker and Records truly is my middle name, as Casey Stengel once said, 'You could look it up!' But you won't, I know you…"

And he kept it up like that, song after song. Chris was right; it was some show. The guys doing radio in Memphis were good, but this guy was different. I couldn't imagine where he was getting all the stuff he was doing. Later he took phone calls from listeners and called it "Boogie Check". The people calling in were very happy to be on the radio, and Landecker was happy to give them grief and cut them off. He seemed to be flying on air, above the radio. It was fast and full of energy, and it seemed impossible to do, for me anyway.

I listened and wondered how I could get better. Then I wondered about Angie and what I should say to her now. And I wondered about Coy and how I should act the next time he wanted to try to buy beer. I didn't have good answers for any of it. When I realized I had nodded off to sleep at least a couple times, I pulled my earpiece out and switched off the radio. And again, I realized that I wasn't worrying about footsteps in the hallway and quickly went back to sleep.

Chapter 13

I heard someone banging on the backdoor and pulled open the curtain of my bedroom to check the driveway. Ben's Mustang was there. I rolled over and put on pants and a T-shirt to go let him in. Ginny and I were sleeping late while Momma was at the store.

"What?" I asked Ben as I opened the door.

"Dumbass Coy, that's what," he said, and motioned for me to step outside. "Sounds like he went to Boonie's and bought beer. Then he got caught."

"What do you mean he got caught?" I asked.

"He got caught. He got sick after drinking all that shit and tried to tell his parents that it was something he ate. He needs a ride. They won't let him drive. He really screwed up." Ben said. "He told me you two were together...that you went to the dump."

I explained to Ben what happened at the dump and that was all I knew, except that he tried to get me to stop at Boonie's with him, and I wouldn't go.

"You want to go with me to get him?" Ben asked. I told him I would and went back inside to change shirts and tell Ginny I was leaving.

"I'm going with Ben," I yelled through the door. "You need to get up and go to the store."

"That's not fair," she yelled back.

"Get somebody to take you to the pool," I said. "Momma will let you go. She always does."

"It's not fair," she repeated.

"Bye," I said and left to go with Ben.

"I should have done more to keep him away from Boonies," I told Ben as he drove.

"Could have been worse,' Ben answered. "Could have been the police that caught him, or he could have wrecked the truck."

Yeah, he could have wrecked the truck and hurt himself, killed himself or somebody else, I thought. It would have been horrible, that much worse than my father's wreck. I tried to put the image out of my mind, but I couldn't. I was getting angry thinking about Coy with his beer driving that truck. I was plenty mad by the time we got to his house.

Coy popped out of the front door the second Ben pulled into his driveway. He was smiling as he crawled into the back seat.

"I am in deep shit," he announced to Ben and me.

"Why did you go back?" I shot back. "Why did you go to Boonies, you dumbass," I said. Ben looked over at me, surprised by my anger.

Coy got mad in a second. "You could have gone too, you chicken shit," he said.

"So you're proud of it?" I asked. "Who drove? Did you drive your truck home?" I asked Coy.

"Somebody did. I might have. I don't remember," he answered. "I was at the dump drinking beer, and then I was home. That's about what I remember. Momma was crying, and Daddy was yelling about taking my truck back. I don't know what else happened," he said, and started laughing.

"That shit's not funny," I yelled at him.

"Well, it kind of is," he said.

"Just like driving off a bridge drunk is kind of funny," I said.

That's when he stopped talking. None of us said anything else until we got to the drugstore. Coy went inside. Ben hung back and waited for him to go inside.

"Your dad, your dad had been drinking when he went off the bridge?" Ben asked me.

"Of course he had been drinking. He was always drinking. He was drunk," I said, trying not to cry.

"I'm sorry Neil. I guess I should have known," Ben said.

"Why should you have known?" I answered. "I didn't tell anybody. I wouldn't tell anybody how bad it was. I expected something to happen. I wasn't surprised." I thought about telling him that I had prayed for it to happen, but I didn't. I knew it would be hard for him—for anyone who had not been through it—to understand.

"I'll talk to Coy about it if you want me too," he said, trying to be the peacemaker.

"I'll talk to him later. I called him a dumbass, not you."

"Yeah, okay. I've got to get to work," Ben said.

I asked Ben if Angie was working today. He said he would check and asked me if I was coming inside the drugstore. I told him I would wait by the car. I didn't want to talk to Coy yet. Ben was gone for a couple of minutes. When he came back out he told me she would be in later. He also told me that Coy was sorry for what he said.

"I told you I would talk to him," I said to Ben.

"He brought it up. I don't think he knew Neil. I don't think anybody knew it was that bad. I'm sorry," he said.

I was sure right then that I was going to cry, so I walked away before it happened. I didn't know if I was right or wrong to have jumped on Coy like I did, but I couldn't stop.

Now, I was the one who was the most upset by what happened, at least I thought I was.

I walked over to Sonny's to kill some time until Chris got to the radio station. I got a coke and sat over in the corner by the window. There were two or three tables full of men eating lunch and talking nearby. These were men who own businesses on the square, or worked nearby. There were also a couple of farmers who had come into town to get some things and had stopped off to eat.

I could hear most of what they were saying. There was a little talk about the presidential election. One of them said he couldn't go Democratic anymore since Wallace got shot. Another one said he didn't particularly like Nixon, but he had done an okay job and he would vote for him again. They talked a little about the St. Louis Cardinals. The Cardinals were our team in Harper's Junction and they had been in the World Series three times in the last few years. They weren't winning as much this year, and the men couldn't understand it. They talked about the old timers they grew up watching and imagined that they would be doing a better job than the boys playing now. I wasn't surprised by any of it. It was all the kind of stuff you heard at Sonny's.

Then one of them, a man who owned a hardware store on the square, said something about the new road about to be built that would bypass the square. He said it looked like the work was starting, and he didn't like the way it had been handled.

"I don't approve of how the route was picked. Who decided?" he asked the others.

"We've been over and over this," a man who owned a furniture store on the square said. "The state decided. It's a state road. They decided."

"Who is they?" the man complaining asked the other.

"I think you know who 'they' is," the hardware store man said. "It's that goddamn Ed Taylor."

I knew the name. Ed Taylor was a politician from Harper's Junction. He represented the county at the state capital in Nashville.

"You don't know that, and you shouldn't say it," one of the farmers at the table told the man.

"I do know it, as sure as I'm sitting here. He's into it, him and his buddy sold that land for the road to the state."

"He didn't own the land," the farmer said.

"Didn't have to. All he had to do was put the road over there, and he was going to get his money," he said. "You know that's how it works."

"I don't know it, and you don't know it either," the farmer said, and got up to leave.

"Have it your way," the man doing the accusing said as the farmer walked away.

"I will, by god," he answered, and walked out of the door.

The rest of the men got quiet after the exchange between the two. It took a couple of minutes before one said something about how much it had rained, and they all talked about that for a while. They sounded relieved to be talking about something other than the new road. I sat and listened for a while longer. No one mentioned the road again as the talk slowed down, and the men began to leave. The last man left at the table was the one who owned the hardware store. He looked over at me and nodded.

"You're Lois' boy aren't you?" he asked.

"Yes sir," I said. "I'm Neil."

"I was sorry to hear about your daddy," he said. "Very hard to lose your daddy, especially at your age." I didn't answer.

"How is your momma?" he asked.

"She's all right, I think."

"You have a sister too, right?"

"Ginny," I answered.

"Tough on a little girl, hard on the whole family," he said.

It was hard on the whole family when he was alive, I thought, but I didn't say it.

"I knew your momma growing up. She was two years behind me in school. Pretty girl, everybody liked her. I haven't seen her much since she married."

That was something I had heard before, people asking about my mother, and then saying that they didn't see her much. My mother didn't socialize. My father wasn't interested in being around other people in town, and it rubbed off on her. She didn't get out. She kept the store, and stayed home. She didn't really have friends, and that was because of him.

"You tell Lois that Johnny Scott said hello. If y'all need anything, you know where my store is," he said, and got up to leave.

"Yes sir," I said. "I will."

I hadn't thought much about my mother and what her life would be like after what happened. Woody and this man had both commented about how pretty she was and how well liked she was. I guess it was true—no reason for them to make it up. And she was still pretty, and she wasn't that old. It made me wonder if she might ever have a boyfriend, or something like it. It was hard to imagine, for me anyway.

I waited until almost two o'clock and walked over to WHJ. Woody was sitting up front at Mrs. Burns' desk when I walked in.

"Ready to get back at it?' he asked when he saw me.

"Yeah, I think so," I said. "I've been practicing a lot, using the tape recorder." I wanted him to know that I knew I needed to get better.

"That's the right way to go about it," he said. "Keep working at it and we'll get you back doing the news soon enough."

There it was. He was telling me that I couldn't read the news on the air until I got better. I couldn't blame him, but it was hard to hear. I would have to have his approval now before he would consider giving me Chris' job. And the thing was, I didn't know how long I had before he was leaving. I wondered if Woody knew.

I said okay and walked back to the control room. I checked inside through the glass door and tried not to look as disappointed as I felt when I stepped inside. Chris glanced up at me.

"Hey, you want to do three to five today? I'll do the news," he said.

"Yeah, okay," I answered. "I talked to Woody. He pretty much said I had to get a lot better before I could do the news again." I expected Chris to take my side, or at least sound sympathetic. He didn't.

"Well, practice," Chris said. "You've got to keep after it if you want to get there. You know, if you really want to do this. Do you want to do this?" he asked me. I was surprised by the question.

"Sure I do," I answered.

"Well, make it happen. You got this far. You keep at it; you'll get there. There's no trick to it. Nobody up here was born to do this. You learn and you practice, and you'll probably get better. That's the deal. There have been two or three people who came through here since I've been here who aren't here anymore. They pretty much came here to play, thought it was all fun, so they didn't work at it, didn't try. Now they're gone."

I don't know why he chose to tell me all that, and I should have thanked him for saying it, but I didn't. I figured he was right though, the people who made it at this job must have taken it seriously and worked pretty hard at it. I thought I had been working pretty hard, but maybe not. I knew I could work harder. I just had to make myself do it.

I picked my music and studied the log. I ran everything through my head several times and even made notes. And my time on the air was okay, no major screw-ups at least. I kept everything going and tried to find new things to say about the songs, and about what was happening in Harper's Junction. I wanted to sound happy about being on the radio.

Chris came in to do the news and finish the shift. I stuck around and listened to him reading the local news. When he was done, I got his old copy and recorded it for myself in the production room. I listened back to what I had done, thought about how to make what I had done sound better, and recorded it again. I did that several times. I glanced over at Chris a couple of times between the recordings, and he nodded his approval at what I was doing.

One of the stories Chris had read for his local newscast—one that I had been practicing with—was about an investigation into the road being built around Harper's

Junction. It said the attorney general's office in Tennessee was looking into possible misconduct in the selection of the route for the road. The story had come from the wire service. Chris had pulled it off the wire just before five o'clock and put it on the air. It stuck out to me because of what I had heard earlier in the day at Sonny's Café. No names were mentioned in the story. It did say the investigation was ongoing and that it was possible that charges would be filed at some point. I knew it was big news, especially if someone around Harper's Junction was being investigated.

I was still in the production room when I noticed the phone line to the control room start blinking. Chris picked it up, and I looked over at him from the production room. He listened on the phone for a few moments and then began to shake his head. He was getting mad. He wasn't talking. He was just holding the phone out from his ear and shaking his head. After a minute or two, he slammed the phone down and walked around to the production room. He walked in and gestured at me to hand him the news copy back.

"Fuck him," he said. "Fuck Woody Lawson. I can't believe what he just said to me." I started to ask him what was going on, but I didn't get the chance. "You better finish my shift," he said, and walked out. I went over to the control room and sat down in front of the board. Chris' record was finishing and it caught me off guard. I grabbed a cart and slammed it in the machine so we wouldn't have any dead air. I didn't have time to announce anything, and I wasn't sure what music he wanted me to play, so I opened the door and called out for Chris. I figured he was sitting down the hall someplace. When he didn't answer, I walked quickly to the front door and looked around for him. He was gone. I hoped he had just stepped out to cool off.

An hour went by and still no Chris. I was worried. WHJ was scheduled to sign off the air at sunset, and I didn't know how to shut the place down. The transmitter had to be switched off, and I wasn't going to mess with that. Luckily the phone rang. It was Woody looking for Chris. I told him I hadn't seen him since they talked before.

"Where is he?" Woody was mad. "Where did he go?"

"He didn't say. I don't know," I answered. Woody muttered a few cuss words.

"Are you okay?" he asked.

"I guess so, but I don't know how to sign off," I answered.

"I'll be up there by then," he said, and hung up the phone.

Woody came bursting in just before sign off and motioned for me to move out of the way. He recited the sign off announcement from memory and started a tape recording of the national anthem. While the anthem played, he pointed to a switch on the far right of a panel that controlled the station's transmitter.

"This one," he said, "it turns the transmitter off at night and on in the morning." The anthem ended, and he told me to flip the switch. "See that," he said, pointing to a rotary dial on the panel. "Now dial one and look at the reading to make sure the transmitter is off." I turned the dial and he nodded." See, it didn't move. We're off the air," he said. 'Now, what did Chris say?' he asked me.

"All he said was I better do his shift and he left."

"That's it?"

I said it was, leaving off the part about what he said

about him.

"I'm surprised he would just walk out of here," Woody said. "You better call me in the morning. I need to find out what's going on with him." I said I would. Woody locked up the station and we left.

I guess I could have asked Woody for a ride home, but I didn't. I walked around to the south side of the square and turned for home. It was nearly dark and things were starting to cool off a little. It was a nice evening for the twenty-minute walk to our house, and it gave me time to think. I wondered why Woody didn't tell me anything about what he and Chris had argued about, or why he thought Chris would walk out of the station like he did.

Momma and Ginny were sitting on the couch watching *The Carol Burnett Show* when I got home. Momma told me there were leftovers on the stove. I got some food and sat down on the chair beside the couch to watch TV and eat. Momma asked me about my day, and I told her what happened with Chris. She seemed surprised too, and she asked me what I thought it would mean if Chris didn't come back.

"I don't know if Woody would give me his job right now or not," I said. I hadn't told her about what he had said about me not being ready to read the news.

"What would stop you?" she asked. I lied and said I didn't know. I should have told her the truth right there, but I didn't. "You've been working pretty hard on this," she said. "I don't see why you couldn't start now."

"I'm not sure if he thinks I'm ready," I said, trying to explain things without telling her everything I knew.

"I think you are, and if you're not you will be soon," she said, trying to sound supportive. I don't know if she believed it or not, but I appreciated her saying it. I didn't say anything else about it.

We sat and watched Carol Burnett for a while before Momma spoke again. She looked at me for a few seconds, then looked over at Ginny and said,

"I hate to say this, but we need to talk about moving." Ginny teared-up immediately and I tried not to. I wanted to support Momma and not make things worse, but I was finding it easier to cry these days, and I was having a hard time holding it back. To give up our house after everything that had happened seemed so unfair. I figured nothing could be done about it, but Ginny wasn't ready to give up.

"Momma, there's got to be something you can do," she said, crying hard now.

"I wish there was. I just don't know what else to do. We don't have the money to stay here. That's all I know," she explained. "Maybe we can figure something out later. We can stay with your grandmother for a while, then get a place of our own later," she said.

"I don't want another place," Ginny screamed. "This is our house. This is my house, and I'm not leaving!" Momma reached over to put her arm around her, and Ginny pulled away.

"It's going to be all right," was all she was able to say.

Maybe it was going to be all right, but it didn't feel that way. It was sure going to be different. I knew that much. We all liked Nana, but I had never considered living in her house full time. She would have rules in the house, and we would have to consider them. There would be two bosses, her and Momma, and that would be a strain. I didn't argue with my mother about it. It's not what she wanted to do either. I felt bad for her, and I felt worse for Ginny. I felt bad for myself too. I was starting to figure out that getting away from Daddy was not going to be easy, even after he was dead.

The phone rang and Ginny jumped up from the couch to get it. She always thought, or at least hoped, the phone was for her.

"Neil!" she nearly yelled when she found out it was for me. I was surprised to hear Woody's voice on the phone when I picked it up. He told me that he wasn't going to be able to work things out with Chris. I didn't know what to say, so I just said okay. Then he told me he was going to get Barry to work Chris' weekday shift for now. "I want you to start working weekends," he told me. "Then if things work out, you can start doing the weekday shift later." I told him that was fine with me, and I thanked him.

"So we'll start you Saturday morning by yourself, then you'll need to come in Sunday morning and work with Barry. He'll have to show you everything that goes on Sunday. It's different with the church services and all." Woody was speaking to me like I knew Barry. I knew what I had seen and heard. It wasn't much. A lot of people were afraid of him. I knew that, and he did a look little scary with the hair and beard, the loud car, and the army clothes.

I finished talking to Woody and then explained to my mother what he had said. She seemed pleased that I was going to be starting a real job, even if it was just on the weekends. She told me that I could still help around the store during the week, at least until I got more hours at the radio station. I didn't answer. I had hoped the radio station job would get me out of the store for good, but I knew she was right.

I told her about Barry. She told me she had been friends with his older sister in school, and that she knew Barry when he was a boy.

"I hate what happened to him," she said. "His best friend too. People say he's not right since it happened. Who would be?"

"Well, I've got to work with him Sunday," I said. "I hope he's not too crazy."

"I don't know, but I don't imagine he's crazy-crazy," she said. "I don't think he would have a job up there if he was that messed up."

So, I was a little disappointed and a little happy too. I had a paying job at the WHJ, but it was not the job that I thought I would get a few weeks ago. I went to bed with my radio on and my earplug in place. I tuned around to a couple of Memphis stations, on to the rock-and-roll station I could get out of Nashville, and finally over to Chicago and WLS. I listened knowing that, at least in a small way, I would soon be one of them. I was a guy who was going to get paid to talk on the radio. I wanted to get started.

Chapter 14

I was days away from my sixteenth birthday. I had to get ready for the driver's test. I also had to go by the radio station to get a station key and to get one last lesson on how to operate the transmitter before I started work on Saturday. It was a lot to think about, along with the prospect of moving out of our house soon. I was also thinking about asking Angie out once I turned sixteen. I kept hearing about the big concert coming up in Memphis on the radio. I imagined getting tickets for Angie and me, and how impressed she would be if I made that happen. But I didn't have the money for the tickets, and I wasn't one hundred percent sure I would be driving by that time. I expected to pass the driver's test, but that hadn't happened yet.

I spent a couple of hours helping out at the store—stocking shelves and carrying out boxes—ate some lunch, and then started walking towards the square. I hoped to see Angie at the drugstore and then go by the radio station. I wanted her to know that I was starting a real job at the station tomorrow. I would try to say it without sounding like I was bragging, and maybe I could find some way to bring up the concert in Memphis and get her reaction to the idea of going.

I put my earpiece in and turned on the radio as I walked. The Memphis station was playing Heart of Gold. It was a song I had played on WHJ while working for Chris. I wondered about him and what had happened with Woody. I wanted to find out more, but I didn't want to get too involved either. It was way too early for me to be taking sides in something like that, but I owed Chris a lot, and whatever happened wasn't good. Chris had done a good job at WHJ. That much was for sure, and it sounded like it ended in a bad way.

Angie was behind the soda fountain when I walked in the front door of the drugstore. Her hair was pulled back and tied behind her head, and she was wearing a white blouse, a different one than she had worn at the river. I saw her before she saw me, and I was able to watch her a couple of moments without looking like I was staring. Of course I was staring. I felt like I could have stood there and watched her all day.

"Neil!" she said, and smiled when she saw me. I smiled back and searched for the right thing to say. I wanted to blurt out how good it was to see her and how good she looked, but I didn't. Instead, I awkwardly blurted out that I was going over to the radio station later to get a key.

"You're getting your own key?" she said.

"Yep, I start work tomorrow."

"That's great, Neil. That's really great."

"I hope so," I said.

"It is. I know it is," she said, and she sounded sure of herself, like she pretty much always did.

I told her that the job was just on the weekends for now, and explained about Chris walking out the other day. She got very interested.

"He read a story about the bypass and then quit?" she asked.

"I don't know exactly what happened. I think Woody called him and said something that really upset him. He didn't tell me, and Woody hasn't told me. I don't know what to think."

"You haven't talked to Chris?"

"No, I guess I should, but I'm just starting, and I don't need to get in the middle of whatever happened with him and

Woody. Not now anyway."

"That is strange though," Angie said. "Who would have said something about what Chris read, other than Ed Taylor?"

Angie had jumped way ahead of me. The story kind of put Harper's Junction in a bad light, but I hadn't thought about someone other than Woody saying something about it. Now I wondered. What she said kind of made sense. The men at Sonny's Café had said something about it too. What did they know about what was going on?

"Please don't say anything about what happened to Chris," I told Angie. "I'll try to talk to him if I get a chance, but I don't want to start spreading this story around because I don't know what happened. Chris might have said something really bad to Woody. I don't know."

"But you want to know, right?"

"I guess I want to know, but there's not anything I can do about it right now. I just want to start this job, make a little money and I need to get my driver's license so I can have a car to drive," I said.

Angie looked at me like she was a little disappointed, but she didn't say anything else about it. I guess I could have sounded a little more upset about what happened to Chris and a little more interested in what might have been behind it, but I didn't. I sounded more like someone who was more concerned about himself, and I suppose I was. I wanted to talk about something else with Angie and not leave things like they felt.

"I was thinking about getting tickets for that concert at the Liberty Bowl," I said.

"I didn't know that," she said, and she sounded surprised. "I'm going."

"You're going?" Now I was the one who sounded surprised.

"Yeah, there's a bunch of us going," she said, and mentioned the names of two other girls and three boys. The boys were all a year older than us. I heard her say it, and I felt sick. I should have asked her to go before now. Worse, I didn't know what to think or what to do. I tried not to show her how I felt, but maybe I should have. I said something I really didn't mean instead.

"Well, that should be fun," I said.

"Yeah, I've never been to a big concert like that," she said, her eyes lighting up. I didn't have anything left to say. I wanted to get away.

"I've got to get to the radio station," I said abruptly. Angie didn't say anything. She just nodded, and I think she sensed that I was upset by what she had just told me.

I walked over to the radio station muttering to myself. I thought things were going a certain way with Angie and me. At least I hoped they were, and now I didn't know. Maybe she just wanted to be friends the whole time. She was interested in the radio thing. Maybe it was never much more than that. I headed up the steps and opened the door to the radio station. Mrs. Burns heard me coming and was looking up from her desk when I stepped in.

"So, you're starting to work tomorrow," she said.

"I think so," I said.

"You better more than think so," she repeated. "I'm going to need your social security number, that is if you want to get paid."

"I do, I mean, I'll get it," I said. "I don't have it with me."

"Well, get it and bring it to me Monday. And you'll have to fill out a time card," she said. "I keep them in the control room. It will have your name on it. You fill it out every day you work. If you don't fill it out, you won't get paid. I'm not going to try to figure out when you worked. You write it down. Got it?"

"Got it," I answered.

"Good."

I stood there a little bit longer, because I couldn't tell if she was finished with me or not. She looked down at the paper on her desk, and when she didn't look back up, I figured it was okay to walk away. I was wrong.

"And one more thing. Don't leave a mess in the bathroom. I don't want to find a mess in the bathroom on Monday morning. You boys can clean up after yourselves," she ordered. I tried not to smile at that one, but I guess I did smile a little. She tried to keep a stern face, but she cracked a little too. I was happy to see it, because she did sound funny, motherly I guess, talking about keeping the bathroom clean. I looked at her for a couple of seconds before she dismissed me with "that's it." I smiled again and went in to see Woody. He was sitting at his typewriter, with a cigarette hanging off his lip.

"Sit down," he said out of the corner of his mouth and kept typing for a couple of minutes while I waited. When he stopped, he pulled the paper from the typewriter, pulled the cigarette out of his mouth, and turned to face me. "I've got a key in here someplace," he said and opened a side drawer to his desk. "You need to keep up with this key," he said. "And just because you have a key doesn't mean you can be in the radio station at any time, understand?" I nodded. "You can be here when you're working. That's it. And you've got to remember to lock the door behind you on the weekends and in the evenings. That means when you're in here by yourself and after you leave. Don't forget to lock the door." I told him I would remember.

"Barry will be up here Sunday morning. You need to meet him at six, and let him tell you everything that goes on," Woody said. "We've got preachers on tape and we've got the live broadcast from First Baptist. We have to get that stuff right or they won't like it. They all pay good money to be on the radio," he explained. I dreaded listening to that stuff, but it was a paying job and it would help get me started.

"So, you're okay with tomorrow morning, right? Except for the transmitter?"

"I think so," I answered.

"Let's go back and go over it." I followed Woody to the control room. Billy was on the air. I didn't bother speaking to him, because I knew he wouldn't answer anyway. I did look over at him and he never looked up.

Woody went over the transmitter controls. "It's pretty simple really," he explained. "You remember the switch that turned the transmitter off? It's the same one that turns it on. Off–On," he said, and pretended to flip the switch. "This dial shows the readings on the transmitter. One is wattage, two is voltage, and three is percentage of power. One, two, three." He went through the readings and wrote them down on a paper form he called the transmitter log. "We do this every hour," he said.

"I've seen Chris do it," I said, and Woody frowned.

"Yeah Chris," he repeated, and continued. "If anything goes wrong, or you have a question, you call me. That's my number right there," he said, pointing to a number written in red ink and taped above the control room board.

"Okay, I will," I answered.

I left with the station key tucked away in my pocket and started for home. I looked across the square to the drugstore and thought about going back to see Angie again, or maybe trying to get a ride with Coy or Ben, but decided against it and walked on. It hadn't gone well with Angie earlier, and I needed to figure out what to do next. I wanted to know more about her plans for the concert and how that all happened. I figured I could find out from Ben and Coy.

As I walked, I started going over what I had to do in the morning, my first day on my own at the radio station. I had practiced a lot and listened a lot, so I didn't expect it to be hard to keep things going. I did wonder what I would say between songs and all the rest for six straight hours. I started going through song titles in my head and trying to come up with catchy things to say, but they all sounded pretty dumb. I would just have to wait and see what came into my mind in the morning.

The wind picked up and the tops of the trees began to sway. I walked fast, hoping to beat the rain. I hadn't noticed how dark the skies behind me had gotten and now it felt like a summer shower was right on top of me. I smelled the rain before I felt it and began to run down the street toward the store. A few large drops began to fall around me when I heard the beep of a car horn coming up alongside me. It was Ben in the delivery truck. He gestured for me to get inside.

"I saw you on the square and figured you were walking home," he said

"Yeah, thanks," I answered. "Angie told me she was

going to the concert at the Liberty Bowl with some friends. Did she tell you anything about that?"

"A lot," he said. "She's been talking about it non-stop at the drugstore.

"Who set it up?" I asked.

"I think she did. She told some girlfriends that she wanted to go, and they talked to some boys about going. I think she started it." I didn't ask anything else. I didn't want to know any more details. We pulled up to the store, and Ben asked me if I wanted to do something later.

"I'm working in the morning," I said, "starting at six."

"Six in the morning? Not this kid. Good luck," he said, smiling.

Ginny, Nana, and Momma were sitting around the front counter when I walked in the store. The rain was coming down hard and it wasn't likely we would have any customers for a while. Most of the people who traded with us walked to the store from their homes in the neighborhood. They wouldn't be coming out in this. I got a coke and a bag of chips and stood by the front window, watching the rain. Nana asked me about work. I told her I was starting in the morning and showed her my key to the radio station. My mother said she would set her alarm and give me a ride in the morning. Nana reminded me that I could be driving her old Ford soon. I told her I was counting the days.

Despite what happened to our father, to us having to move soon, and Angie going on a date with someone else, I was happy about the job and looking forward to starting work the next day. I was going to do a radio show that would be all mine, and in just a few days I would be driving myself in a car that I could call my own. It didn't make all things right, but it felt better.

Chapter 15

I don't remember when I finally went to sleep. I switched back and forth between listening to the radio and just lying there, staring out the window. I lost track of time, but it felt like it had only been minutes between the time I fell asleep and when I heard a knock at my door.

"Neil, time to get up and get going." I was in a fog, but I was able to figure out that it was my mother. It took me another second or two to remember why she was getting me up when it was still dark. I must have gone back to sleep, when I heard her again.

"Neil, now," she said more urgently than before. "You can't be late on your first day." *No, you can't be late at all when you're signing on a radio station*, I thought. *There would be nothing but dead air.*

I popped up and threw on some blue jeans and my favorite t-shirt. I grabbed a sweet roll from the kitchen and followed my mother out to the car.

"Have you got your key?" she asked. I nodded and she smiled. "Well, you're on your way then. Are you nervous?"

"Not really," I answered. I don't think I was awake enough to be nervous yet.

My mother dropped me off in front of the station just as the sky on the far side of the square began to show light from behind the row of old buildings. I paused for a moment to look up at the control room window and then climbed the dark stairs to the locked door of the radio station. I pulled out my key and fumbled with it for a minute before I was able to open the door and step inside. I looked around for a switch and turned on the lights to the front office and the hallway. I looked over to check the clock. It was ten until six. I had a few minutes to pick out some songs and get ready. I went inside the bathroom first thing and tried to pee, but I couldn't yet. I looked over at the coffee pot and thought about Woody. I imagined him making coffee at about this time every workday morning.

I reached inside the control room and flipped on the lights. I looked around and tried to get things straight in my head. As I went over all the buttons and switches, it hit me how quiet the room was. Without radio going on and no one else around, all the soundproofing made it almost completely silent inside. Standing inside with no music, or news, or commercials playing, the only sound I could hear was the soft hum of the big electric clock above the control room board.

I had an idea for my first song of the morning, so I pulled a record from the oldies rack and cued it up. I grabbed two carts, one with the national anthem and another with a WHJ singing jingle, and slid them into the machines to my right. I got out the notebook that contained copy used every day on WHJ and opened it to the sign-on announcement. I looked out the window of the control room and checked the big thermometer that hung just outside the glass. It was seventy-one degrees and the sky to the east had gotten quite a bit lighter in the last few minutes.

At about thirty seconds before six o'clock. I stepped around to the transmitter controls and watched the seconds count up to the top of the hour. When the second hand hit twelve, I hit the transmitter switch and watched the needle on the little monitor window jump all the way to the right. I jumped back around and hit the green start button on the far right cart machine. A drum roll started and a Marine Band version of the national anthem barked out through the speakers in the control room. WHJ was on the air and I was in control–kind of.

I sat down and put on the headphones for the first time as a paid radio announcer and waited for the anthem to end. I glanced out the window and saw the orange morning sun peak over the buildings as the horns blared out the final line of the anthem. My hand was trembling a little as I switched on the microphone.

"WHJ radio now signs on the air for another day of broadcast activity. WHJ is owned and operated by the Mid-South Broadcasting Company and operates on an assigned frequency of 1410 kilohertz with a transmitting power of 1000 watts." The words all came out of my mouth, and in the right order too. It was an okay start, I thought. I reached over and punched the start button on the second cart machine just as I finished the announcement.

"WHJ...Harper's Junction!" the recorded singers' voices jumped out at me in my headphones. They were plenty alive and ready to go at 6:00 a.m. I hit the turntable switch and heard the first few notes of my first song of the morning rise up in my ears.

"Morning has broken Harper's Junction, and there's no need to fix it. Things are looking pretty good from where I sit. I'm Neil Robinson and this is Cat Stevens on WHJ!"

I was off and running, and the time flew by. It felt like I had very little time between songs to do much. I can't remember anything particularly clever I had to say, but there were no big mistakes, no clumps of dead air, and no one called to complain. And there were no local newscasts on Saturday morning—a great relief. It felt like a victory and that was good enough. I was happy and surprised when my last hour came around. I realized shortly before noon that I was suddenly very tired. The adrenalin had worn off, and the short night's sleep had caught up with me. Billy came in right at noon. I put the network news on at noon, and the control room door opened. I got up and stepped away from the board. He brushed by me and said "hey," and that's all. I walked down the hall and out the door—making sure to lock the door behind me—and bolted down the steps and out the front door.

I crossed the street and walked up on the courthouse lawn. I turned and looked up at the WHJ control room window, and it made me smile. I felt good about what just happened.

I crossed over and went behind the drugstore to see whose cars were there. I didn't want to see Angie, but I did want to see Ben and Coy if they were working. Coy's old truck was the only one parked out back, so I stepped inside the back entrance. I heard WHJ playing softly somewhere in the rear of the pharmacy when I walked in. I looked over to my left and caught the eye of Ben's father who was standing in his spot behind and above the back counter. He was counting out pills.

"Neil!" he said very loudly when he saw me. "I was just listening to you. Ben told me you would be on the radio today, so I turned it on back here. You did a wonderful job, son."

I should have just said thank-you, but I couldn't think to do that.

"Well, I'm kind of just starting," I said. "I think I'll get better." I must have sounded like I was apologizing for something that I really didn't intend to apologize for.

"Well of course you'll get better," he said, "but you're

off to a good start already. I can tell you that."

"I hope so," I said. "I think I'm going to like it."

"If you like a job, then you will give yourself every chance to get better," he said to me.

"I appreciate that, Mr. Geist," I said.

"Coy's up front," he said, and went back to counting pills.

"I heard you. It wasn't terrible," Coy said when he saw me.

"But it wasn't that good either, was it?" I asked.

"You said that," he answered, and smiled.

"I've been thinking about the concert. You want to go? You, me, and Ben, why not?" I asked him.

"Yeah, well, why not," Coy said. "Ben will be here in a couple of hours. I'll talk to him."

And just like that, it felt like everything between us was okay, as it should have been.

I walked home, replaying everything I had said on the radio. I could remember it all. Some of it sounded better in my head than other parts of it. Then I thought about having to go down and work with Barry in the morning. I wasn't looking forward to that. It made me more than a little anxious. I also figured it wouldn't be a lot of fun playing tapes of preachers and church services. It was the job though, and they were going to pay me for it.

The house was empty when I got home. Momma and Ginny were at the store. I went back to my room to lie down and put my earpiece in to listen to the radio. I was asleep in minutes. Momma and Ginny were home when I woke up from my nap. I could hear the television. I got up and went into the kitchen. Momma had left some food on the stove for me. I made a plate of pork chops, mashed potatoes, and slaw, and sat down at the table. Momma came in and sat down too. I told all about my shift at the radio station, and she seemed happier than I could remember.

"6:00 a.m. tomorrow morning, right?" she asked, and smiled.

"Yeah," I answered.

"I'll set my alarm. You said Barry will be up there with you?"

"Yeah, I don't know what all goes on up there on Sunday morning. It's a bunch of church programs and preachers. He's suppose to show me what to do," I told her. "I'm not sure about him. People think he's a little crazy."

"You shouldn't worry about Barry," she said. "I've known him all my life. His sister is one of nicest people I grew up with and he was a good boy too. He couldn't have changed all that much."

I wondered. A lot of what I had heard about Vietnam was about boys who came back changed. And it looked—at least from a distance—like Barry had changed too.

I finished supper and called Ben to see if he wanted to get out for a while. I was wide-awake from my nap, and I knew I wouldn't be able to get back to sleep until late. I told Momma I was going to ride around with Ben for a while, and she didn't like it. She reminded me that she was the one who was going to have to get me up in the morning. I told her that would not be any trouble, but I knew that might not be true. I saw the lights from Ben's Mustang shine up from behind the house and went out to meet him.

"Coy said he would try to get out tonight, if his parent's let him." Ben said when I got in. "You two are okay, right?"

"Yeah, we're okay," I answered. And we were.

Ben made the usual loops around town, and we saw the usual folks.

"Somebody said there is something going on out behind the box factory," Ben said. "And it's not the dump crowd."

Kids were always looking for new places to stop their cars and hang out without being bothered. Sooner or later the police would find out and come around. When that happened, kids moved on. The box factory had been shut down for years, and there were no houses near it. I remembered there was a big open shed behind the main building. I told Ben that's where we might find them. He drove us out to south edge of town and pulled in slowly behind the box factory's old main building. I remembered what happened behind the dump and told Ben to turn his lights off. He looked at me funny, but switched them off anyway and crept along the gravel drive to the back of the building. Through the darkness I could see the outlines of several cars under the shed, and I could see the glow of lit cigarettes near the front of the cars. I hoped we had found the right place.

"Who the hell is that?" someone yelled out to us.

"Looks like Geist," someone else said. Ben's car was easy to recognize. He was the only kid in high school with a Mustang. I was relieved that someone from the dark had recognized us and that it was a group of kids. Ben stopped the car, and we got out. This was a different bunch from the ones Coy and I had seen behind the dump. There were no football players, and there were no girls, just a bunch of guys—some with cigarettes and a couple with beers. They were the smarter, older kids from the high school. Several of them had just graduated.

"Robinson," one of them called me by name, and I thought I recognized the voice from out of the dark. It was Chris. He was sitting on the hood of the old Rambler he drove. He was holding a can of beer and smoking a cigarette. I walked over to him, and he offered me a beer and cigarette right away. I didn't take either one.

"I heard you on the radio today," he said, and he sounded a little funny. I figured it was the beer. He paused and nodded his head. "Not too bad," he added. I told him thanks and wondered if I should ask him what happened. Turns out I didn't have to.

"Woody Lawson told me not to read any more stories about the road, or about Ed Taylor, or anything else that sounded like news. Fuck him. It is news. If that's not news, what is?"

"What did you say to him?" I asked Chris.

"I told him it was chicken shit, and he told me if that's how I felt about it I could leave. I was leaving anyway, so I left," Chris said. "You just need to know the kind of guy you're working for. Chicken shit."

"You think it was him talking or someone else?" I asked.

"Yeah, I've thought about that. What if someone else told him not to talk about it? We're supposed to be telling people what's going on. What if some of these guys are breaking the law? Who's going to do something about it? We could at least talk about it, you know?" Chris explained.

I didn't answer, but it seemed like it wasn't that simple, that it wouldn't be easy for someone like Woody to say bad things on the radio about Ed Taylor or anyone else like him in Harper's Junction. Chris had told me that my job at WHJ would be to say good things about Harper's Junction, and I know he remembered that. He wanted something different from it now though, and he wasn't going to get it.

"I want to be a lawyer," Chris said, "to help clean up shit like this." He said it and looked away. I looked away too. He was clearly upset at the way things had ended. He wanted to leave the radio station and go off to school, but he didn't want to leave this way. He wouldn't look back at me after he said it, and I knew it was time to go.

"See ya," I said. He didn't answer.

I motioned to Ben for us to go, and we walked to the car.

"What did Chris say?' Ben asked.

"I think he told me to watch what I say on the radio if I want to keep working there."

"So that's what you'll do." Ben said, and I couldn't tell if he was asking or telling me.

"Guess so."

"You want to try and find Coy?" he asked.

"I better get home and try to go to sleep," I said.

"Six, right?"

"Yeah, six. You want to give me a wake-up call?"

"Right, you wait for my wake-up call and you'll be waiting a real long time."

I stayed up late again. I was unsure about the deal with Barry at the radio station in the morning, and the thought was keeping me awake. I watched TV until two channels signed off, and there was nothing left to watch except an old movie that I didn't like. I got in bed well past midnight and still couldn't sleep. I thought about what Chris said, but I couldn't get too worked up about it. I hadn't even considered working at a radio station until a few weeks ago. I didn't have any strong feelings about what we should or shouldn't say on air. Chris had worked at WHJ for over two years, and he had thought about it. Me, I wanted the job, and I needed the job if I wanted to get out of the grocery store and have my own money to spend. It was that simple in my mind.

Chapter 16

I don't remember going to sleep, but when I heard my mother's voice I tried to get up right away. I had been surprised yesterday morning by the early hour, but it wasn't as much of a shock today. "I'm up," I said, and pulled myself to the edge of the bed. I heard my mother click on the light in the kitchen as I sat and tried to make my brain work. I pulled on my jeans again from yesterday and got a clean shirt out to wear. I put on my tennis shoes and stumbled out to the kitchen. Weekend sign-on shifts were going to take a lot of getting used to.

My mother had made a ham sandwich for me. I put the sandwich and a sweet roll into a paper sack and followed her out to the car.

"Tell Barry I said hello," my mother said to me, as she drove. "I haven't talked to him in years, probably not since his sister moved to Memphis." She didn't know that he had said the same thing to me about her.

"Okay," I told her, but I must have not sounded like I would.

"Neil, tell Barry I said hi," she repeated. "Tell him to stop by the store sometime and say hello. I'd love to see him." I wasn't sure about saying all that to this guy I didn't know and wasn't sure I should trust.

The radio station was still dark when I got there. I went inside, turned on the lights, and walked back to the control room. It was about ten minutes until six. I sat in front of the board and looked out the window as the sun crept up from behind the row of buildings on the east side of the square. The clock ticked up towards six and there was still no Barry. I looked at the log and saw the name of a program listed as "The Master's Voice", but I had no clue about where it was or how to get it on the air.

I was getting more nervous by the second. It was three minutes until six when I looked up at the red phone number above the board and reached over for the phone to call Woody to ask him what to do. At the moment I picked up the phone and started to dial, I heard the loud screech of brakes outside. I set the phone down and looked outside. Barry's old hot rod was sitting down below. He was already out of the car and in the building. I heard heavy steps hitting in quick succession up the stairs, followed by a moment or two of quiet, and then the outside door flew open and banged against the wall. I barely had time to move before Barry stepped into the control room.

"Move!" he shouted. "Why did you lock the door?" I kind of shook my head. "Where's the tape?" he asked. Again, I had no answer. He spun around and grabbed a reel-to-reel tape from a shelf underneath the turntable, and in what looked like one quick motion, slapped the tape on the playback machine and threaded it onto an empty reel. He turned a small switch on the machine to the right and hit the play button. At first sound, he stopped the tape and pulled it back a couple of inches. He did all of that in about fifteen seconds.

"You know how to turn this thing on?" he said, pointing to the transmitter controls. I nodded yes. "Fire it up then." I walked over and hit the switch. Barry hit the microphone a moment later and recited the sign-on message from memory, before starting the tape. "This is the Master's Voice" came blaring out of the speakers above the board. Barry turned the monitor almost all the way down to where you could barely hear the program and swiveled around in the control room chair to face me.

"Did you tell Lois I said hello?" he asked, and pulled a pack of Marlboro's out the front pocket of the green Army jacket with his friend's name on it.

"I think I did," I lied.

"Sorry to hear about your daddy," he said, surprising me. "That's hard, losing somebody like that." I waited for him to say something else about it, but he didn't.

"How is your Momma?" he asked, but he didn't wait for an answer. "You know I had a crush on her when I was a little boy. She was so pretty and nice."

"She told me to tell you hello. Said you ought to come by and see her," I told him, and felt funny saying it.

"She said that? Well, that's what I'll do. She working in the store?"

"Every day, except Sundays."

Barry turned, looked out the window, and smoked his cigarette without saying anything else for a while. It gave me a couple of minutes to look more closely at him. He had fairly long sideburns and hair that came down below his collar. A thick beard covered most of his face. He was wearing blue jeans, a white T-shirt, an Army jacket, and some old boots that looked like they were Army issue too. I figured Barry was still in his twenties, but he looked much older. He seemed to be lost in thought, so I stood and waited without talking.

"So, what do you need to know?" he said after a while. "What do you need to know about this?" he asked, referring to the Sunday morning shift.

"If you would just go over everything," I said. "I've never been up here on Sunday morning."

"That's what I'll do then," he told me, and started

to go through all the programs I would have to play. "It's all church shit," he said, taking me by surprise. "This thing," he said, nodding at the tape, "lasts half an hour, and that's good. It gives you time for a shit and a smoke first thing." He went on from there, running down the programs and showing me where to find them.

"The last thing you've got is First Baptist. It's live and it comes through here," he said, pointing at the dial on the board. "Don't screw up First Baptist, cause if you do you'll hear about it. And they won't be too forgiving over it. I can tell you that from experience."

"I'll try not to," I said.

"Yeah, well, I was up pretty much all night so I'm gonna take my tired ass down to the car. If you need me, I'll be right there, sleeping," he said, nodding down his parking spot on the square. I said okay, but I would have liked it better if he had stayed and watched me do all this. He left, and I watched him from the window. He took off his jacket and stretched out in the front seat of his car. He put the jacket over him and appeared to go right to sleep.

I stumbled through the shift. I believe I got everything on that was supposed to be on. It was clunky in spots, and there was a little dead air here and there, but it was okay. At least no one called to complain. I was coming up on eleven o'clock and The First Baptist broadcast. It made me a little uptight, thinking about what Barry had said about not messing this up. At three minutes before the hour, Barry startled me by showing back up, this time without making a sound. I hadn't heard him come in, and he was standing right behind me before I noticed. He must have seen me jump when I noticed him, and if it had been one of my friends I would have said something about not sneaking up on me.

"Just thought I would check on you. We don't want to get blamed for screwing with the Baptists," he said, and smiled for the first time. He talked me through it, and we got the service on just as it should have been. "Now you've got about fifty minutes," Barry explained. "It's a crappy shift, but it's pretty easy." Barry pulled out a cigarette, lit it, and leaned up against the turntable cabinet.

"I told Woody I would do the afternoon shift until you, or somebody else, was ready to do it. And I will, but I don't want to do it for very long. I can't be locked up in here for too long. I'm telling you this because if you want the job, you need to get ready," he said to me. I told him that I appreciated him letting me know. He continued looking out the window.

"This is really none of my business, Neil, and I didn't really know your daddy, but I know he liked to drink, and I do too. I used to see him out. I was in the Army too, you know, like your daddy. Different time, different place, but maybe not so different either. I saw shit and did shit that's hard to believe happened. He might have seen things like that," Barry said, and paused again. "Something to think about. You lose somebody like that, and it might not ever make sense. I don't know. I lost my best friend, and I know that will never make sense."

He paused for a few seconds and added, "I don't know a goddamn thing really." He said it and left. I heard his tires squeal when he pulled out from in front of the radio station.

I thought about what he said and I was glad he said it. At least it gave me something to think about other than me praying for Daddy to die before he ran off that bridge.

Chapter 17

I got my driver's license on the Wednesday after my 16th birthday. My mother closed the store for a couple of hours and took me down to the highway patrol station in my grandmother's car to take the tests. I got through the written test and walked out towards my grandmother's car to get ready to drive. I expected the trooper on duty to follow me out for the driving test, instead my mother came out of the small building and got in the car on the driver's side.

"I told Bobby you knew how to drive, and he sent me out here with this," she said, and handed me a small green card with my name, address, height and weight typed on the front. It was my driver's license. She knew the trooper, and he didn't want to bother riding around with me, so he sent the two of us on our way.

"Congratulations," she said, and grinned at me. "Just be careful driving. Promise me that. You know how dangerous the roads can be." I did know, and I promised her that I wouldn't go crazy with the car.

"I've got to get back to the store," she told me, and I drove us there, careful to mind the speed limit and all the traffic signs.

"You okay with me taking a drive around?" I asked her when we pulled up beside the store.

"Sure, don't be gone too long, and remember what I said."

"Be careful," I repeated. She smiled and told me she loved me.

It was hard to believe. I pulled away from the store

driving by myself in a car I could almost call my own. I imagined all the places I could go. The list was endless. And I thought about the places I could drive away from—those places I could leave behind. And curiously, I found myself driving towards one of them. I drove out to the highway and turned onto the river road. Within minutes of getting my driver's license, I pulled up onto the bridge where my life had changed in a shocking way only a few weeks earlier. I stopped to look down into the brown water, but I didn't stay there long, and I didn't shake.

I drove on down to the river and parked near the willow trees. I sat with the window rolled down and smelled the river breeze. It smelled cleaner, and the water was less brown, more a dark green. And even though I felt like I had blown it with Angie, it was still a perfect spot. I did imagine her sitting in my car, with the white blouse and the warm smile. And even if it didn't happen with her, I decided it would happen—that I would kiss a girl in this spot. I promised myself that I wouldn't let a moment like that pass again. I thought about the possibilities—the car, the job, and our last two years of high school, and I felt a little better. It was fear that had held me back, and I needed to get past it. It had started with my father, and I felt it in everything I did. He was gone, and it was time to let that fear go.

Epilogue

Barry hung on to the job at the radio station for a couple of months. He decided he had to leave when the first hint of fall arrived, and he sensed the change in the seasons. I knew this because I started to get to know him and like him. He told you what he thought, and I always got the feeling he was trying to be honest with what he said. Good to his word, he had stopped by to see my mother, and they decided very quickly that they liked each other's company. He started helping her too; he would put up stock and clean up around the store while he was there. It started slowly and built into something more. My mother began to make excuses to get out of the house in the evenings and on the weekends. Ginny and I both knew she was going to see Barry, and even though we didn't talk about it, I don't think either one of us had a problem with it. She was happier, and that meant the most to us. They eventually dropped the pretense, and Barry started spending more time with the three of us. I grew to appreciate how he treated my sister and me, as well as our mother.

Barry was also the first person I finally told about my prayer. He told me that he had prayed a lot in the Army. He prayed for the strength to kill people—people he didn't even know and didn't have any problem with, other than the fact that some of them wanted to kill him. And most importantly, he had prayed for his best friend to live the day he was shot in Vietnam, but he didn't.

He told me that my prayers had nothing to do with my father and that bridge. He said he didn't have the power to save his friend, and I didn't have the power to kill my father. And even so, he told me I was right to do everything in my power to protect my family and myself. That's what I liked to believe, and it was a relief to have him say it to me.

And I found out he and Boonie were good buddies. Barry told me that Boonie had lost a buddy in the army too, and that he was the only person in town that he could talk to about it. He said he thought it was important to be able talk about these things. I took it to mean I should do the same.

I got the everyday job at WHJ after Barry left, and a couple of months later I was sleeping in what used to be my uncle's bedroom in my grandmother's house. The house thing turned out to be okay, not great, but okay. We learned to ignore most of Nana's rules, and she finally gave up on a lot of them herself.

Angie and I never kissed. She started dating the boy she went to the concert with. We did stay friends, but I always wondered what would have happened if we had kissed that day down by the river. After high school, she went off to college and studied journalism. I know she chose that career to help satisfy her curiosity about the world. She wanted to make a job out of finding out about new things.

Chris did study law and eventually became a lawyer. I hope he got to change some things in a way he had in mind. Ben went back to Chicago to go to college and took a high-paying job in finance there after finishing school. Coy and I attended college closer to home and roomed together. That lasted a couple of years, before we made new friends and started to grow apart a little bit. After college, Coy came back to Harper's Junction to teach school.

And I've spent more time than I would have liked thinking about what happened on that bridge—about my father's death, and about my mother and I acting as if we could put it all behind us. Maybe she did, but I doubt it. I never have. I think about him every day, and some days I choose to forgive him, but on other days I can't. I do wonder how things would have turned out if he had lived. My prayer was answered, but that doesn't keep me from wishing it could have been different, and from imagining a life that would have gotten better without him dying.